MW01153518

The First Year It Sleeps

Brenda Gibrall

Copyright © Brenda Gibrall 2019
All rights reserved.

The First Year It Sleeps **is a work of fiction.**
Names, characters, places, and incidents are products of the author's imagination or used fictitiously.

Cover Design by Mary Gibrall Scott

Chapters

. . . *and a little child shall lead them.*

Isaiah 11:6

Chapter 1

Kate Henry

AUGUST, 1955, WAS NO HOTTER OR DRIER than any August of any year in Chesterfield County, Virginia, but it seemed so to me. For weeks there had been no rain, no relief for the parched earth surrounding our house. Even the rambling rose bush climbing the trellis by our side porch had turned to papier mâché, its scarlet blossoms hanging earthward. Fissures in the hardened soil had divided the lawn into puzzle-like pieces, an occasional patch of clover pushing through its cracks here and there. It reminded me of my Grandma Gallagher's antique Belleek tea cups resting in the kitchen cabinet downstairs, their delicate shamrocks now crackled and crazed. While the teacups were reminders of her life in Ireland, the rose bush was a marker in time for my sister Karena and me. When asked why she chose the fragile teacups to place among her few articles of clothing on her voyage to America, my grandmother would say, "To remember, just to remember." For me, the rose bush was a reminder of my dad's departure for Korea. But for Karena, my little sister, it was a symbol of her first attempt at being a savior.

In the spring of 1950, just before joining his Marine unit in Korea, our father planted the rambler at the foot of the trellis he had built against our side porch. Hearing the thud of the shovel as our father tore away at the clay-like soil, Mrs. Angstrom, our next-door neighbor, peeked around the corner of her house to see what was going on. Seeing my father, my sister, and me tending the soil and the delicate plant, Mrs. Angstrom sighed in admiration.

"Ah, Jim," she said. "That is a particularly hardy species you have there."

"Yep," my dad said, winking at Karena and me. "What we have here, Mrs. Angstrom, is the newly-developed and only recently-registered American Rose Society hybrid Katie-Karena, the ever-blooming, drought-resistant trellis rose."

"A lovely specimen," said Mrs. Angstrom, going along with his joke while straining to see the bush's classification tag.

Then Mrs. Angstrom moved between my little sister Karena and me, spread her arms across our shoulders and watched as our father tamped the root ball into the dirt. Mrs. Angstrom, the neighborhood rosarian, had schooled us in all the classifications of roses so that at a very young age we knew a floribunda from a grandiflora, a tea rose from a rambler. Her rose garden was planted in her side yard across from our kitchen door where it could get the most sun each day. At least, that was how she had explained it. It was more likely that it was the only spot of earth save the front lawn that her husband, Reverend Angstrom, had not tilled and planted with vegetables of the summer and winter varieties. Whenever we ran out to play, Mrs. Angstrom would educate us on her latest planting, giving the common and botanical names which we would repeat to ourselves over and over in anticipation of the short quiz that would come up the next morning as surely as the sun.

"Patience, girls," Mrs. Angstrom said to my sister and me

as our father christened the baby bush with a fine mist from the garden hose.

"Remember, when it comes to a rambler, the first year it sleeps, the second year it creeps, and the third year it leaps."

And, looking into our anxious faces, she said "When it is time for your father to return home from Korea, this trellis will be heavy with perfumed blossoms."

Karena cut her eyes at me on hearing Mrs. Angstrom's words and I knew exactly what she was thinking. We could do this. We could bring our father home if we only took care of this rosebush.

We watched as the curling green tendrils climbed the trellis frame each summer knowing the greater the number of roses, the fewer the days until we would see our father again. We watched, watered, and counted blossoms until the summer of 1953 when our father, just as Mrs. Angstrom had promised, appeared specter-like at the top of Kildare Avenue, his thin frame wavering against the heat rays rising up behind him from the asphalt, his duffel bag at his side as he walked toward us and away from the war.

In the summer of 1955, Toby, our cocker pup, spent long humid afternoons splayed across our kitchen threshold, his ears draped over golden paws and his black nose pointed like a compass toward the stairway. Panting from the heat, he waited for his cue from Momma to slide across the linoleum, race up the scarred pine stairs to the second floor of our boxy, white Cape Cod and rouse my sister and me from our naps.

We slept fitfully on those humid afternoons, if we slept at

all, our heads and clothes drenched with perspiration. No cooling breezes blew through the screens, the white ruffled curtains standing stiff as columns beside each windowsill. Lying there in the stillness, I listened for the familiar and predictable sounds of summer afternoons on our street, a way of knowing the time without looking at a clock and when our rest periods would be over. First was the sound of the mail truck grinding to a stop at the end of our driveway, the snap of the mailbox door, and the spray of gravel as the truck pulled away. Next was a locomotive running the rails behind our neighborhood, signaling with a piercing whistle as it neared Branch Creek Road, a warning to cars approaching the crossing and a sign to us that nap time would soon be over. Our house was so close to the track, in fact, that the rattle of the trains that kept us from sleeping when we first moved in became a soothing lullaby that literally rocked us to sleep. The warning whistle as the train approached the crossing and the engine light that flickered through our bedroom windows at night became comfortably predictable, a reassurance that all was well and that our lives were in sync with the rhythms of the world. Listening for those sounds, I would inhale deeply, enjoying the sweet scent of jasmine seeping through the screen. And some days, despite the uncomfortable heat, I would drift off to sleep.

From noon until dusk, the lawns along our street were mostly empty of children and the cooling waters of nearby Pocahontas Lake were off limits. All public places were suspect, even the ones that brought us relief from the heat. A deadly virus, our parents warned us, may be lurking in the lake's dark depths or carried to us through the crowds mingling there. Rest in the afternoon became the regimen. As invisible to us as the Cold War that sent us diving under our school desks as air raid sirens screamed overhead and imaginary Russian planes, heavy with bombs, flew above, polio sent us to our rooms each summer afternoon - out of the heat, out of the crowds, and out of danger - to melt into our beds.

At the beginning of the summer, one of our classmates was stricken, leaving him in an iron lung and his parents awash in a sea of what-ifs and whys. His two sisters, one older, one younger, peered through the door of the children's ward at the Medical College of Virginia where, unable to breathe on his own, Paul lay encased in a tubular machine, his lungs no better than dried-out sponges, his diaphragm muscle paralyzed by the virus. Like fireplace bellows, the sealed iron lung expanded and compressed his lungs for him, pulling breath in and forcing it out. His words, when he could speak, came only as the air was pushed through his voice box. In his eyes, though, his sisters saw resilience, determination, and more courage than the two of them could muster.

As if put on notice, our parents became even more rigid in their insistence that rest and isolation would stave off the virus. In the dog days of August, 1955, outdoor play was reserved for the coolness of evenings, the stars and moon lighting our way, fireflies and mosquitoes our constant companions. There were five of us who met on my front stoop each evening eager to plan that night's adventure. By the end of August, there were only four.

Chapter 2
Branch Creek Farms

BRANCH CREEK FARMS, the neighborhood where we lived, had been a prosperous tobacco farm since before the Civil War. In the mid 1940's, most of the farm's acreage, which lay across the railroad tracks from its manor, was sold to the Veterans Administration so that a much-needed facility for wounded veterans could be built there. In 1946, McGuire Veterans Hospital first opened its doors. The remainder of the farm behind the manor was sold to a real estate developer who divided it into boxy lots where he built white-shingled Cape Cods and small brick ranchers, many becoming first homes for families of GI's returning from World War II. Our family was no exception. Like other families who had lived in multi-generational homes, our parents took advantage of the GI bill to buy our first home, leaving the security and comfort of Grandma and Grandpa Gallagher's spacious two-story home on West 27th Street in the city to set out on our own in the suburbs.

My few tangible memories of life at my grandparents' house in the city were often awakened by simple things like the smell of yeast bread rising on the stove, the graceful flutter of sheets across a backyard clothesline, or a mimosa blossom like the one that brushed its silky threads against my second-floor bedroom window there. Whenever I saw a stately white-haired lady dressed in lavender heading out for church or a small-framed man, sleeves rolled up, suspenders in place, walking toward his workshop to repair a broken screen, I was back on West 27th Street, back with my grandparents. With a host of cousins living in the house across the street, I felt grounded and linked to my surroundings, comfortable in my setting. It was the intangible feelings of comfort, security, and belonging that I would come to miss the most and work to replicate once we moved from there.

My mother's three sisters, each of whom married, stayed with our grandparents as we had, and then eventually moved to homes of their own, had thrown a housewarming party in our new living room the Sunday after we moved in. The new house smells of freshly painted walls and shellacked wood floors greeted them as soon as they walked through the front door. Mom welcomed each as they entered, Karena and I taking their packages and stacking them in front of the Morris chair. Aunt Marian, the oldest Gallagher sister, nodded with approval as she looked around our new home and then moved toward the couch, taking the center seat. Her two younger sisters, Elizabeth and Marguerite, followed suit, nodding also with approval and offering congratulations as they moved to sit on either side of her. Cleo, their much-loved sister-in-law, sat on a chair pulled in from the kitchen, her West Virginia twang enriching every clever and humorous comment she made. Doris, Mom's best friend she met while working at Kresge's Five & Dime, was the last to arrive and sat next to Cleo on the hassock.

In her slim navy dress, her wavy dark hair resting on her shoulders and a white rosebud corsage pinned to her collar, my mother looked as lovely that day as she did in the black and white wedding photo of her and Dad on the end table beside her. Sliding to the front edge of the Morris chair, she looked down at the brightly-wrapped boxes, her dark eyes glistening in anticipation as she unwrapped each one, finding towels, sheets, pots and pans, dishware, and all the things she would need to set up housekeeping. Her favorite of them all was a pressure cooker from Grandma Henry, my dad's mother, that hissed on top of our stove many a winter day filled with Mom's delicious recipe for Brunswick Stew. Our next-door neighbor, Reverend Angstrom, would provide the chicken from his hen house as well as corn, potatoes, celery, tomatoes, and carrots from his garden. The other ingredients, like Worcestershire sauce, bouillon cubes, and spices, were available at Accashian's Market on Branch Creek Road as well as, true to Southern cooking, that tablespoon of sugar needed to sweeten and de-acidify the tomatoes. And of course, it was served with sweet, warm Southern cornbread slathered in butter.

Amid the din of laughter and animated conversations, strawberry punch was ladled from Grandma Henry's cut-glass punch bowl into the matching cups that were hanging by clips along its rim. Cucumber tea sandwiches, cream cheese and date bread squares, frozen fruit salad, and fresh melon balls filled platters and bowls on a card table Karena and I set up in the dining room, a white Battenberg lace cloth disguising its worn, crayoned surface. And of course, for dessert there was Aunt Cleo's much-loved Pearl's Pound Cake, heavy with almond and vanilla flavoring, the toasty surface as crunchy as the inside was smooth. Anticipation of the life we would lead filled up the house, spilling into the yard and out into the streets, which, as we were among the first to move in, were still hard-packed clay in want of a generous coating of asphalt.

Karena and I were spellbound by the animated, clever, slightly suggestive jokes told by our aunts, jokes that Karena and I giggled at without understanding a word. Laughter, like sadness, is, after all, contagious.

"A young man goes into a drugstore," began Aunt Elizabeth, "and asks the clerk for three one-pound boxes of chocolates for his date that evening. Looking puzzled, the clerk asked why the young man didn't just buy a three-pound box of chocolates. The young man replied that if the young lady let him hold her hand, he would give her one box of chocolates; if she let him put his arm around her, he would give her a second box; and if she let him kiss her, he would give her the third box.

"The clerk looked at him and said, 'Sounds as if you have a big evening planned. Are you sure you don't want to buy some rubbers?'

"'Oh, no,' said the young man. 'If it rains, I'm not going.'"

Side-splitting laughter erupted from our aunts and so we laughed, too, without understanding why, quietly though, as we were hiding within earshot but out of their view in the stairwell.

Not to be outdone, Aunt Cleo with perfect comedic timing and expression began:

"An old man walks up to a brothel and knocks on the door. The Madam opens the door, takes one look at the old man and says, 'Get out of here, old man. You've had it!' To which the old man stammered, 'Oh, oh, I have? Well, then how much do I owe you?'"

Again, a gale of laughter.

Karena looked at me quizzically and whispered quietly, "What's a brothel?" Holding my forefinger across my lips while pressing my other hand across hers, I shook my head and mouthed, "I don't know." Her eyes rolled upward as if she were thinking when she mouthed back at me, "I've got a good one," and before I could stop her, she slipped down the stairs startling the aunties saying loudly, "Knock, knock!"

The aunts tried to hide their surprise and amusement at seeing Karena standing before them attempting to join in the joke telling.

"Knock, knock," said Karena again, showing some exasperation at no one answering her question.

Aunt Marguerite took the bait saying, "Who's there?"

"A little old lady. . ."

"A little old lady who," said Aunt Marguerite, grinning and knowing what was to come.

"Oh, Aunt Marguerite, I didn't know you knew how to yodel," said Karena, slapping her hand on her thigh as she threw her head back and laughed.

Maybe one more, the expression on her face said as she tilted her head to one side. Mom, seeing there was no end in sight, cupped her hands over the ends of the chair's armrests preparing to pull forward and stand.

"Knock, knock," Karena said looking at Aunt Cleo.

"Who's there?"

"Jamaica," replied Karena.

"Jamaica who?" asked Aunt Cleo.

"Jamaica call to your momma today?"

With that our momma stood and made a call to Karena, a nonverbal one, her arm raised and finger pointed up the steps from which Karena had come all the while trying to suppress her own laughter lest she show approval to Karena for her antics. We were sent to our rooms, giggling with each step because we could still hear the ladies laughing downstairs.

When we were old enough, we learned to ride our bikes, a grocery list in Momma's Palmer-perfect handwriting stuffed in a back pocket, up Lancaster Avenue to Harry Accashian's Market on Branch Creek Road, buying only what would fit into the wire baskets on the front of our bikes. Some days this would mean making more than one trip or enlisting a neighbor to ride along and help carry the packages home, the reward for them a package of candy Camel cigarettes, which they sucked on, blowing the powdery coating into the air like smoke.

For shopping downtown at Thalhimer's or Miller & Rhoads Department Stores, Momma, Karena, and I would walk the two miles past the Veterans Hospital over the county line into the city where the bus line began. It was a long time before our mothers would let any of us take the bus into town alone.

One day, Momma and Mrs. Tinsley, our next-door neighbor, worn down by our pleading, agreed to let me and Charlene, or "Charlie" as we called her, give it a try. It didn't come without a long list of instructions and reminders on how and when to transfer to the cross-town bus, not the one headed for the east end of the city, and then catch the downtown express, exiting at Sixth and Broad Streets. Whatever Momma forgot, Mrs. Tinsley filled in, both focused on what seemed to us as endless minutiae on how to travel by bus. As soon as the laundry list of what to do was completed and they had handed us our bus tokens, Charlie and I flew out the front door and started our two-mile trek toward the bus stop just over the county line into the city.

Climbing the steps onto the bus, we dumped our tokens into the fare box and asked the driver for transfer tickets for the crosstown bus and the downtown express. Excitedly, I walked toward the back row of seats knowing how much fun we had on our school bus, a group of us across the back seat singing songs and telling jokes, but Charlie grabbed the back of my shirt, pulling me toward the front saying, "We need to sit behind the driver so we can be sure and get off at the right stop." Once we got to our seats, two rows behind the driver, she said softly, "Dummy, the back rows are for the Negroes who ride the bus. We shouldn't sit back there and they *can't* sit up here. How did you not know?" Charlie *always* knew the rules and even how to break them at times. I, on the other hand, knew the rules *most* of the time and, if I did, tried not to break them.

As we got close to Sixth and Broad, Charlie pulled the bell cord over the window to let the driver know we wanted to get off at the next stop. We had made it.

There was a new-found confidence in our gait as we descended the bus and walked purposefully through the double doors of Miller & Rhoads, past the cosmetics counter where the Charles of the Ritz lady smoothed foundation on a middle-aged lady leaning across the counter. We headed down the creaking wood floor to stand beneath the ornate gold clock angled out over the hall, the clock an often-designated meeting place for friends. Stepping on the escalator, we headed up to the Tea Room where a fashion show was in progress. Peeking through the door, we saw models prancing down the runway to tunes played by Eddie Weaver on the organ as ladies wearing hats and heels lunched together at tables beside the runway.

Leaving the Tea Room, we headed for the teen department, running our fingers across the racks jammed with hangers holding Villager and McMullen blouses, Bermuda shorts in madras plaid, a table of neatly folded and carefully arranged neck scarves nearby. Mostly I studied the styles so that my mother could sew up something similar for a fraction of the cost. Instead of Villager labels in my blouses, there was just the tiny dot of blood from a pin prick my mother always seemed to leave on an armhole seam, a seam which required many straight pins inserted side by side along the sleeve edge to gather its fullness into the small arc of the armhole before basting it in place. She had mastered this technique; the set-in sleeves of the blouses and dresses she made were always free of unsightly puckers, a tell-tale sign the garment was home-made. To me, that red dot was more valuable than any designer label.

Down two escalators, we visited the basement, the place our mothers always insisted we start our shopping spree. If we couldn't find what we needed there, then we would head for higher floors and higher prices. We always ended our shopping sprees with a hot dog or, if it were a Friday, a tuna salad sandwich in the Thalhimer's basement cafeteria or a grilled cheese at the Murphy's down the block. As it was a Friday, Charlie and I decided on the grilled cheese at Murphy's when our shopping was done. Heading into G. C. Murphy's, we looked toward the counter only to see our mothers sitting there on stools drinking coffee, heads together in conversation, giggling like two school girls. Charlie looked at me and then cleared her throat loudly just as we came up behind them.

"Ahem," Charlie said.

When they did not respond, we tapped them each on the shoulders. Stunned, our mothers swiveled toward us and saw our disappointed faces staring back at them. They each giggled, amused at our expressions and at their being caught checking up on us.

"Don't be upset," Momma said. "This trial run gave us the confidence that you two know what you are doing and next time, you can go it alone. Neither of us could have rested knowing you were navigating the bus system with all its stops and transfers to get downtown."

"Tuna salad or grilled cheese?" asked Mrs. Tinsley while grinning at both of us. "Lunch is on us today."

Eventually, Southside Plaza, a new suburban strip mall arose near McGuire Circle with Thalhimer's and J. C. Penney as the anchor stores. Our trips downtown became less frequent as the string of stores near our home had anything we would need. From there we would purchase fabrics and patterns for the clothes our mother made us, records for our record player, or new spring hats to wear for Easter Sunday, our quiet, patient father standing by with his arms folded across his chest as Karena and I tried on bonnet after bonnet or as we looked through the stacks of 45's in the record store.

My sister and I were becoming, in our Grandma Henry's words, young ladies and she often reminded us that "pretty is as pretty does." Behavior unbecoming to a lady would not be tolerated. One Sunday while washing up the lunch dishes, my mother, aunts, and Grandma Henry were discussing a recent event in the neighborhood concerning Mrs. Bell, Grandma Henry's next-door neighbor, and her little dog, Termite. It seems Mrs. Bell's dog nipped at everyone's ankles as they strode down the sidewalks, some bus riders scanning the walkways before stepping off the bus from work, looking for the little varmint. Aunt Gladys, my youngest uncle's bride, was one of Termite's victims. When she stepped off the bus, the little creature nipped her ankle, ripped her new stockings, chewed on the hem of her best work dress, and then, to add insult to injury, raised its leg and peed in the shoe she stepped out of as she tried to get away.

"I was hotter than h-e-double-l," remarked Gladys, spelling the offensive word knowing that Karena and I were all ears.

Always spelling, those ladies. Well, Karena thought, I can spell too. She skipped out the front door, down the front steps, and along the sidewalk singing for all the neighbors,

"I know how to spell
H-e-double-l
Thanks to Mrs. Bell
I know how to spell"

Before I could reach her and, once again, cup my hand over her mouth, my grandmother's phone was ringing. It was Mrs. Bell calling to say her granddaughter's spelling abilities were quite impressive, but maybe she should check on her.

This call may have prevented an even more inappropriate vocabulary/spelling public display when Karena later overhead the aunts speaking in the kitchen about a woman of ill-repute in the town whom folks called a "whore."

"Does that begin with an 'h'?" asked Karena.

That spelling lesson precipitated the first of many lectures about how to become ladies, and not young women of a less-respectable variety.

"Always stand when an adult enters the room, respect your elders, always say 'Ma'am' and 'Sir,' sit with your legs crossed at the ankles, not at the knees. But better to cross them at the knees than to sit spread eagle which is never allowed. Dress should always be modest. Hat and gloves, if going downtown," my grandmother recited repeatedly.

We are always becoming something, I thought. Teenagers, young adults, mature adults, married, divorced, widowed, ill, alcoholic, addicted, homeless, institutionalized, idolized, demonized, victims, victimizers. It all starts with those first memories, a wilting rose bush or a father home from the war. And builds each day, each memory, each heartache, each joy until we become.

Chapter 3

The Manor

BRANCH CREEK MANOR, its residents long gone, sat at the entrance to our neighborhood exuding a history that we chose to see as that of a true Southern plantation. Six massive columns, rising to the roof, lined its front porch. At its center was an ominous-looking front door of solid oak with heavy brass handles and locks. On both sides of the door stood two tall windows with wavy glass panes. Five windows sat across the second floor, the center one perched over the entrance. The structure which once suggested position and prestige had fallen prey to time and the elements. Those who lived there from the 1800's on were buried in a weed-and-tick-infested cemetery near its back door, a hundred-year-old oak tree standing guard over them. Many summer evenings, the five of us - Will, Sonny, Bucky, Charlie, and I - filed through the cemetery's wrought iron gate, playing hide-and-seek among the crumbling, moss-covered headstones. We all knew it was sacred ground, but our need for adventure and our unquenchable curiosity overrode any thought of trespassing in that world. We were both drawn and repelled by our curiosity and fears. Slaves, if there were any, would have been buried there also, but outside the iron fence, along its outer perimeter, yet close enough to serve the family in the next life. Several crumbling footstones rested outside the fence, the names erased by time and weather. Only one was legible, a newer one with flowers cradling it. Charlie and I knelt down and brushed aside pink petals that had fallen across the name: Ida Louise Lawrence, 1898-1953.

"Who's Ida Lawrence?" asked Charlie.

"I don't know, but she can't be one of the owners because she's buried outside the fence," I said. "She wouldn't have been a slave because she was born in 1898. Lincoln had freed the slaves in 1863 before she was even born. I wonder who she was?"

"And somebody must be taking care of her plot. Who could be around to do that? That gives me the willies!" said Charlie with a shiver and then catching herself remarked, "But I'm sure there is a reasonable explanation and we don't need to be afraid of anything."

Turning around, Charlie and I left the graveyard and walked to the front of the manor. Looking into its foreboding façade, I could envision Scarlet O'Hara standing at the massive front windows, peering from behind heavy velvet drapes as she scanned the landscape for Union troops, Prissy standing behind her wide-eyed and trembling with fear. The air was always cooler there in the evenings and smelled sweetly of magnolia blossoms, lavender, and jasmine. And before the moon rose and the frogs began to bellow, the earth was eerily still.

"Oh, my Lord, I think I see her ghost standing at the window. Don't you see her, Charlie? There, to the left of the first window," I said to Charlie as we stood staring into the wavy glass from a comfortable distance in the yard while waiting for the others to start our evening play.

"Ah, come on, Kate," said Charlie. "Your imagination is

running wild again. This is not Tara. This is Branch Creek, a long way from Atlanta. Your head gets so full of images you can't see what is really there! Cool it, will ya!"

Even though Charlie was trying to be tough, I knew she was a little spooked by what we saw or imagined we saw through that window. And when a dark figure, a small Negro girl, crossed behind the window pane holding a lit candle, even Charlie became a believer, grabbing me by the wrist and pulling me toward the roadway.

"Now do you believe me? That was Prissy!" I said to Charlie as I tried to keep up with her long stride as we ran out to the road.

"Believe what?" she asked breathlessly, her eyes wild with fear, her mouth full of denial.

"That this place is haunted, that we saw the ghost of Prissy pass across the window pane," I said.

"Of course not. Don't be ridiculous! *Gone With the Wind* was just a movie. Prissy and Scarlet were not real people, just characters in a book."

"I know you saw what I saw through that window. Why else would you drag me away?" I said gasping for breath as we barreled down the street.

"Because, because," she said haltingly taking a breath between words, "because we have to meet Will and the others and we're late. They'll think we chickened out. We're the only girls in the group so we have to be braver than any of them. And besides," she said suddenly letting go of my hand and running all the way down Kildare, her words trailing behind her, "I have to peeeeee!"

Scared it right out of you, did it? I thought. *You don't fool me.*

A broken window latch we had discovered made it easy for the five of us to make our way inside the manor, climb the spiral staircase, and rummage through old chests in the attic where we found belt buckles inscribed "CSA" or scraps of worthless Confederate money. Once we even found a blackened silver candlestick hidden beneath a loose floorboard.

Against Branch Creek Manor's massive columned façade, our small white Cape Cods looked like Monopoly houses strewn in front of a large doll house. The once opulent jewel of Southern warmth, charm, and hospitality was now sad, overgrown, and disheveled, a far cry from the grand stature it enjoyed before and after the Civil War. Looking through the front porch columns into its massive windows was like looking into the eyes of an ineffectual "Big Brother" who saw all that happened within the Monopoly pieces spilled across its front lawn, but could do nothing about it. "Tramp," as we called him, lived in what remained of a former caretaker's cottage in a field behind the empty manor, not far from the family cemetery. A tall, muscular Negro, he appeared to be in his mid-twenties. No one knew how he got there or where he came from. Maybe, we thought at the time, he wandered up the railroad tracks behind our neighborhood and decided that this was home. Our parents did not know of Tramp's existence until a tragedy made him known to them as well as everyone else in the county.

Chapter 4

The Tinsleys

IN THE THREE YEARS THAT MY FATHER WAS AWAY, our family and the families of other servicemen in the neighborhood struggled financially and emotionally. When Charles Tinsley, our next-door neighbor, was called to serve on an aircraft carrier out of Portsmouth in 1951, his wife Sylvia, twin daughters Nadine and Nora, and youngest child Charlene, moved in with us in an effort to save on household expenses.

Charlene "Charlie" Tinsley became my best friend. Her sisters, Nadine and Nora, were as delicate as Belgian lace and as dainty as their tiny mother. Each had fine, silky blond hair, deep blue eyes, and perfect petite figures. They brushed their hair a hundred strokes each day until it glistened in the sun and checked themselves carefully in the hall mirror before stepping outside, making sure hems were even, slips were not showing, circle pins were securely fastened on the collars of their blouses, and bobby sox were rolled over just twice, the folded edges resting atop each saddle shoe. Preferred reading for them was not Nancy Drew mysteries, as it was for Charlie and me, or classics like *Little Women*, *Animal Farm,* or *1984*, but glossy movie magazines which they read while sprawled across the living room floor. Turning pages was the extent of their exertion on those hot summer days.

Charlie, on the other hand, was tall for her age with large

angular features, long bony hands and feet and sun-streaked russet hair always pulled back into a stringy pony tail. Like me, she loved to play baseball, fish crayfish out of Branch Creek, and ride her bike at break-neck speed from the top of Kildare Avenue to the bottom where Lancaster Avenue angled in and leveled off the road's surface. And sometimes on those August days, momentary relief from the heat was as simple as that: pedaling our bikes up Kildare, turning around, and flying down again, the humid air rushing across our faces and whipping our hair Medusa-like around our heads. While the younger girls in the neighborhood pushed their doll carriages up and down the short stretch of sidewalk that led from each house to the street and Nadine and Nora preened in front of the teenage boys who passed by, Charlie and I built shanty-style forts out of pine branches or shot marbles with the neighborhood boys. When Mrs. Tinsley had brought newborn Charlene Marie home from the hospital, Mr. Tinsley took to calling her Charlie, a concession Mrs. Tinsley allowed in the hope of softening her husband's disappointment at there being yet another woman in the household.

If ever a man needed a son, it was Mr. Tinsley. He was a sight to behold, a robust man with thinning blonde hair, ruddy complexion, a paunch that required suspenders to keep his pants up, and the ever-present cigar angled in the corner of his mouth. Even on the rare occasion when the cigar was wedged between his index and middle fingers, his smile arced to the left, a brownish liquid oozing from the corner of his mouth. He rolled the cigar from the left to the right side of his mouth, left to right, left to right, over and over again, head tilted back, while pondering a problem or trying to clarify a thought before speaking, catching the cigar midway and clenching it with his teeth when his thought process was done. An avid Notre Dame fan, Mr. Tinsley dreamed of having a son play for Frank Leahy's Fighting Irish. As a child of the depression from a working-class family, college had not been an option for him, but for his son, he would make it happen. He just needed that son. Charlie would have to fill that need, baiting hooks when my dad and Mr. Tinsley went fishing, learning to tie flies for his collection of fly rods, and working with him during the summer in his new business.

On his return from duty on the aircraft carrier, Mr. Tinsley decided to quit his manager's job at an A&P grocery store in the city and start his own business, Tinsley's Rolling Market, a sort of 7-Eleven on wheels. In the summer, Charlie spent the mornings riding with her father in his rolling market, going from neighborhood to neighborhood, clanging a large dinner bell to let the housewives know fresh vegetables and cooling snacks were available right in front of their homes. The brown eggs and cresses from our neighbor Reverend Angstrom's garden were a favorite of the ladies on Mr. Tinsley's route. Charlie weighed the produce on a scoop-shaped metal scale that swung from three chains in the rear window of the bus. She kept the cooler stocked with Pepsi Cola, grape Nehi, and orange Tru-Ade. She straightened the softening rows of Babe Ruth and Hershey bars that rested in a box inside the ice cream freezer after neighborhood children had snatched their favorites, scraping the melting chocolate from the candy wrappers as they descended the bus steps and hit the hot pavement. She watched the thermometer on the freezer carefully on those summer days, the lid opening and closing many times as eager little hands reached inside for Popsicles and Eskimo Pies. And in the sweltering heat of August, her father always planned his route so that he could drop Charlie home at lunchtime.

Before my father and Mr. Tinsley returned from the service, our little house bulged at the seams, the number of occupants having gone from three to seven. In spite of the crowded conditions, there was great comfort in knowing that we were not alone in our struggle. We were surprisingly compatible, this household of women. Charlie and I joined our mothers in the evenings after supper dishes were done and laundry was folded for long, loudly-contested games of Canasta on our screened porch, an ever-present pitcher of sweet iced tea and wooden bowls of peanuts and butter mints at hand while Nadine and Nora lazed away in the living room polishing their nails or rolling each other's hair on plastic rollers. Karena played quietly with the story-book dolls our Grandmother Henry had dressed in hand-crocheted costumes for her, changing their outfits and combing their hair. She, too, played cards – usually a game of Fifty-Two Pick-Up with an unsuspecting younger cousin or friend.

On Sunday mornings, instead of attending Mass at Sacred Heart Church where we were members, our car-less two-family household set out on foot for McGuire Veterans Hospital Chapel where a Catholic Mass was scheduled each Sunday at 9:00. The seven of us walked single file along the busy Branch Creek Road, our heads covered with lace mantillas and shoes shined to perfection. Later in the day, when the weather permitted, we would sometimes change into Bermuda shorts and tennis shoes and return to the hospital carrying boxed suppers of fried chicken, potato salad, cold bottles of Pepsi, and a large army blanket to spread on the lawn. Sitting across from the outdoor court eating our supper, we watched the paraplegics play aggressive games of basketball, their muscular arms doing the work their withered or missing legs had once done, propelling themselves around the court and each other. In spite of their handicaps, the veterans, for the most part, were good-spirited and good sports. A healthy amount of teasing and taunting one another encouraged them to show the other guy, to do their best.

An uneasy feeling always washed over me, though, whenever a wheelchair-bound young man caught my eye; I feared I would see instead my father's crystalline blue eyes, he who was in the midst of battle in Korea and we who were never sure about his welfare in a land of names and sounds exotic and unfamiliar to us. Letters from him were scarce. The rare ones we got were cherished and read over and over again, until the words moved from the page into our memory. As my father crested the hill of Kildare in 1953, we were overjoyed to see his weary face, but in my heart, as he drew us near, I knew a piece of Korea remained within him.

Chapter 5

The Angstroms

WILL ANGSTROM, the son of a self-ordained Baptist preacher, lived in the Cape Cod next door. His dad, Miles, was a preacher on Sunday and an accountant the rest of the week. His real passion, though, was farming. Even though his lot was only a half-acre, to him it was a thousand-acre farm where he grew giant gourds and golden squash, bright red tomatoes, the yellowest corn, the greenest pole beans and cresses, and the brightest, tangiest raspberries that wiggled through his chicken wire fence drooping over into our yard.

"I don't know about this," I said to Charlie one day as we crept, hunched over, our heads down, along the low fence that separated my yard from the Angstrom's while keeping our eyes on the luscious ripe raspberries. Charlie was filling a small plastic pail with tender berries, tugging at the branches along the fence with such vigor that the fence undulated from post to post.

"I'm not sure we should be doing this, Charlie. It is stealing, isn't it? Well, isn't it?"

"For Pete's sake, Kate, pipe down. Who do you think you are anyway, Sgt. Joe Friday?" said Charlie as she threw another handful of raspberries into her bucket. "If you're really worried about it, just eat the ones that fall into your yard. Even Sgt. Friday would tell you that. If it falls in your yard, or hangs over the fence, it's yours," she said.

"I don't think that applies when you're bending the branch

over the fence!" I said turning to leave.

"That's so like you, Kate. It's always the letter of the law instead of the spirit. Can't you ever have any fun? Geez!"

Climbing into bed that evening, I examined my conscience by going over the day's events as I had been taught, blessing myself with raspberry-stained hands. If it were a sin to take the fruit from the ground, it was probably only venial, I thought to myself as I recited an Act of Contrition just in case before drifting off to sleep.

Not having a mule or a tractor, Mr. Angstrom, wearing denim overalls, a white, starched, long-sleeve shirt, and a wide-brimmed straw hat, pushed a cumbersome wooden plow up and down his backyard each spring, forcing the plow's head deep into the dirt making rows for each vegetable he was to plant. He was not a big man. Watching him push that plow blade through the contrary county soil was a study in determination, of mind over matter. He would always remind us as we watched him that the first row was the most important. If it were straight, the ones to follow it would also be straight. But, if it curved, all the rows would curve. This lesson was not lost on his congregation. He prepared the souls of his church the same way he prepared his garden soil, working them and it over and over, row by row, until their texture was just right and their souls and the soil were ready for seed.

"Timing is everything," he would say of both endeavors, pointing his index finger skyward. "Timing, patience, and vigilance."

With the help of his sons, George and Will, Mr. Angstrom had built his tin-roofed chicken coop out of cinder blocks at the back of his lot where his hens laid large brown eggs and his rooster woke us up each morning. George and Will, who like their father were small in stature, were strong in body and faith, and more times than not a credit to their upbringing. Mr. Angstrom loved his Lord, his wife Helen, his sons, and his country, but, given the day, not always in that order. He teased the neighborhood kids lovingly, carved fancy whistles for them out of the gourds he grew, and prayed hard for the Catholics who lived next door because surely, dear Lord, they were going to hell.

Will, the younger son, had his father's playful sense of humor and his mother's love of the arts. He played the piano faithfully each summer day under his mother's watchful eye. If she left his side to stir a pot of stew on the stove or to answer a phone call, Will would mischievously play a raucous boogie-woogie that brought his mother back to her post next to the metronome. Through the living room window, I could see Mrs. Angstrom standing over him just before noon on those summer days, her long slender fingers resting over her narrow hips, her food-splattered white apron tied snugly around her waist while the metronome on the piano ticked languidly away in the humid, still air. Mrs. Angstrom, even when cooking and cleaning, looked as if she could be ready for church just by taking off her apron. She always wore stockings with clunky high heels that laced up to her ankles, her gray-streaked hair lying in soft curls around her face. She was, in her demeanor and all her dealings, the poster girl for preachers' wives.

When he was done with practicing, Will, with large sheets

of blank newsprint tucked underarm and grease pencils in hand, climbed the stairs to his bedroom, perched at his window seat, drew his knees up, pressed the soles of his feet flat against the wall, and sketched life as he saw it along Kildare and Lancaster Avenues. He loved the rectilinear lines of the long rows of houses that curved up Lancaster Avenue, houses he sketched with precision, as well as the graceful arcs of the cascading willow trees hanging limp and lifeless in the still August air along Branch Creek. When he tired of drawing, he picked up his Bible, sprawled across the foot of his bed, and dutifully read the Psalms aloud over and over finding the beauty and rhythm of the words as soothing as their message. When he finished with scripture, Will picked up his latest Hardy Boys mystery and followed brothers Frank and Joe on their latest escapade. He was reading the entire Hardy Boys series in order of publication, of course.

Unlike many boys his age, Will's fine motor skills were better than his gross motor skills. I guess you could say he was a little clumsy. During our Saturday ballgames in the spring, Will always rushed to play in the outfield where he prayed the ball away from himself at each crack of the bat.

Oh, Lord, send it Charlie's way this time.

He was a good sport, but not good at sports. I know he didn't mind that we were Catholic, and looking back on it, I don't think his father did either.

One day in May, after we finished up our baseball game, Charlie and I walked into the wooded area across from the ball field looking for wildflowers. There we could usually find Queen Anne's

Lace, Black-Eyed Susans, clusters of wild violets, and rare Lady Slippers so coveted by gardeners. Hearing footsteps in the brush behind us, we turned to see Will, who had followed us into the woods.

"What are you two up to?" he said, his arms folded across his chest, the sun streaming through the trees creating a halo around his golden hair.

"Just picking wildflowers for Kate's May altar," said Charlie with a snippy tone in her voice. She was anticipating his next remark, though, and today she was ready.

"And what's a May altar?" asked Will wrinkling his brow in feigned puzzlement.

Before she had a chance to answer, I began blurting out a litany of information in answer to Will's question.

"You see, Will, many Catholics set up altars in their homes during the month of May in honor of the Blessed Mother," I began exuberantly. "We also have a beautiful May procession at our church where all the little girls who have just made their First Communion wear white organdy dresses, lacy white veils, white patent leather shoes, and lacy socks as they follow the priest and the altar boys into the church where an eighth grade girl chosen by her classmates for her virtue and beauty wears a lovely, long white dress with a soft sky-blue sash and climbs a beribboned ladder to place a crown of tender pink rosebuds on the statue of the Blessed Mother in the sanctuary of the church. I have a May altar set up in my bedroom and I place fresh flowers there regularly in front of my statue of the Blessed Mother. I also have three pairs of Rosary beads, all blessed by the Pope, and five novena cards that I am saying simultaneously, praying for the conversion of Russia and the end of the Cold War. Not only do I have a statue of Mary, I also have statues of St. Joseph and the Sacred Heart of Jesus. You should see 'em" I said breathlessly. "When you turn out the lights, they glow in the dark!"

Charlie threw me an icy stare.

"Isn't that like worshipping idols, those graven images forbidden in the Bible?" Will asked. "I've heard that's what you Catholics do with all the statues of saints in your churches. You kneel before them, light candles to them, and ask them for help as if a marble statue could do anything for you."

Charlie stepped forward and said curtly, "Will, let me see your wallet."

"Why?" asked Will.

"Just - let - me - see – it," she said, her words measured, her teeth clenched.

Will hesitated for a moment and then stuck his thumb and forefinger deep into the back of his denim shorts' pocket and pulled out a fat brown wallet of tooled leather, scenes of bucking broncos and cacti running to its zippered edges.

"Open it," said Charlie.

"Why?' said Will.

"So I can answer your question," said Charlie, rolling her eyes in exasperation.

Slowly and reluctantly, Will unzipped his wallet spreading it open for Charlie to see. Stuck neatly inside plastic sleeves were school pictures of his classmates, a Willie Mays baseball card, and a photo of his grandparents sitting on a porch swing at their farm in the Blue Ridge Mountains with Will tucked in between them.

"Why do you carry these around with you, Will?" asked Charlie.

"Which ones?"

"That one," said Charlie pointing to the baseball card for starters.

Pulling his prized Willie Mays baseball card from its sleeve and holding it high he grinned and said, "No explanation needed for this one. 'The Say Hey Kid' reminds me to keep trying no matter what!"

"And those?" said Charlie looking at his classmates lined up in the sleeves.

"My classmates' pictures?" he asked with a laugh. "To remind me of the funny things they said or the silly things we did."

"And this one?" asked Charlie

Looking down at his grandparents' photo, Will sighed and said, "We lost them both last winter. This reminds me of all the fun I had visiting them during the summer. That's where I learned to tend to chickens and ride a horse."

Charlie took a deep breath and then pointing to Will's grandparents' photo she said, "Our statues are just like those pictures. They are just reminders of the saints, the good lives they lived, and the lessons we learn from them."

Will, still looking at his grandparents' photo, hesitated and then said, "Okay, okay, I get that, but why do you pray to Mary?

That 'Hail, Mary' that you say over and over on that long string of beads, what is that all about?"

"Will, when members of your church are ill, doesn't your dad ask the entire congregation to pray for their recovery? We are just asking the same of Mary, that she 'pray for us now and at the hour of our death.'"

"Hmm," Will sighed and thinking hard said "Okay, I get that too, but what about the priest who speaks Latin mumbo jumbo none of you can understand over a chalice of wafers, genuflecting before it, sprinkling fairy dust over it or whatever he has to do to turn it into the Body and Blood of Christ? You really believe all that hocus-pocus?"

"Gee whiz, Will, don't you Baptists believe in the Bible just as it is written, word for word?" she asked.

"Of course, we do," he said. And this time he was rolling his eyes at her.

"Okay, when Jesus holds up the bread and wine at the Last Supper, He doesn't say 'This *represents* my Body and Blood.' He says 'This *is* my Body and Blood'."

At that, Will threw up his hands, turned on his heel, and walked out of the woods. He was thinking, though.

I stood with my mouth open, stunned at Charlie's responses.

"What," she said, her brow wrinkled, a slight grin on her lips.

"Where did all that come from?" I asked her.

"Mom made us watch Bishop Sheen on TV last night. The same questions came up. Doubt Will and his family saw it," she said, smiling as we walked out of the woods.

The next day, my mother hollered up the stairs to my bedroom that someone had left a package for me on the front stoop. We were used to Mr. Angstrom leaving eggs or squash on our stoop in brown paper bags. My dad had even stepped into a bag of eggs one morning as he was rushing out the door for work, the swear words that issued from his mouth were loudly audible but funny coming from he who never raised his voice, much less swore. My mother, sister, and I tried not to giggle, but the expression on his face as he pulled his foot out of the bag sent us into gales of laughter and my father even began laughing at himself and the egg goop dripping from his shoe.

While this latest gift for me came from the Angstrom's yard, it was not vegetables or eggs. Instead, it was a beautiful bouquet of roses: yellow hybrid teas, sweetly fragrant red floribundas, white and lavender miniatures, and, in the center of the bouquet, one pink "Queen Elizabeth" grandiflora, all of them gathered together with a sky-blue satin ribbon.

"Oh, no," I said to myself as I scooped up the bouquet. "He didn't."

The card simply said, "For your May altar."

Hearing voices coming from the Angstrom's yard, I crossed the hallway from my bedroom to Karena's and peeked out her window. There, in the side yard, was Will standing beside his mother's stripped rosebushes, his chin resting on his chest, his hands shoved into his pockets. Mrs. Angstrom had one hand on her hip and the other hand, finger pointing in the air, within inches of Will's face. Her high-pitched voice became even shriller as she questioned him about why he had cut her prize-winning roses, especially her highly-regarded and much-pampered "Queen Elizabeth." About that time, Mr. Angstrom rounded the corner of the house and went to Will's defense. Will had already confessed to his dad about the roses, about his conversation with Charlie and me. Mr. Angstrom, his preacher hands gesturing as he spoke to calm his wife, told her it was an act of kindness, an act of reconciliation on Will's part.

"Besides," he said, "now you won't have to spend an hour each morning dead-heading your plants. Will did it for you."

Chapter 6

The Goodes

SONNY GOODE, AN ONLY CHILD and younger than the rest of our group, lived across from us near the corner lot at Lancaster and Kildare Avenues where we played baseball each spring. He and his family, immigrants from Hoboken, had arrived in the fall, just in time for Sonny to begin sixth grade at Branch Creek Elementary, where Will and Bucky, the fifth member of our group, were seventh graders. Sonny's dad had answered an ad for work at the DuPont plant located in Chesterfield and moved his family there.

While the Goodes were fond of Southern cooking and appreciated Southern hospitality, those humid Virginia summers could take their toll. On the worst of those summer evenings, the Goodes - Henry, Marie, and Sonny - carried their TV onto the side porch, running an extension cord through the door to an outlet in their living room. Rocking back and forth on a green floral glider, they laughed away the evening with Sid Caesar or sang along with Rosemary Clooney the top ten on "The Hit Parade." On Sunday mornings, as our family and the Tinsleys prepared for Mass at Sacred Heart Catholic Church in Richmond or the chapel at the VA hospital and the Angstroms trooped out to Branch Creek Southern Baptist Church, the Goodes watched Oral Roberts heal the sick and the lame somewhere behind the glass of their television screen.

Sonny was the kid on the block who seemed to have it all if

it could be bought: a fancy English racing bike, a TV, the latest model family car, and a comfortable two-bedroom brick rancher his parents were renting. I always had the feeling, though, that they could be moving on any day. They seemed without roots, somewhat restless, and were not, like most of us, anchored by relatives who lived nearby. "Carpetbaggers," my Grandpa Henry called them.

Mr. Goode was very cordial and loved to talk, talk, talk on any subject whether it was baseball, politics, fishing, hunting, or how to change a piston, or which motor oil was the best. One day I asked my dad to help me with my vocabulary words. I was having trouble remembering the meaning of the word "gregarious." My dad looked at me and said, "Just think of Mr. Goode." "Goode the Gregarious," I thought to myself and never forgot the meaning of the word.

Mrs. Goode was always polite and more reserved in her encounters with the other ladies in the neighborhood. She seemed to be feeling her way cautiously in her new environment, taking in and evaluating all that surrounded her in the new place she would have to call home. I admired her calm and humble presence, her unpretentiousness. She was unflappable in the worst of circumstances. Once, we escorted Sonny home after he gashed his finger on a broken soda bottle. Toby, our cocker spaniel, had mated with another pure-bred cocker in our neighborhood and the owner had offered my dad two of the pups from the litter. Charlie, Sonny, and I watched as my dad examined the pups in our back yard stretching out their long tails across a tree stump. Unbeknownst to Sonny, the tails of cocker pups are trimmed to a stub and my father was about to do the surgery. When his knife came down across the first pup's tail sending it to the ground, Sonny followed suit fainting away into a puddle of his own vomit. He also managed to gash his finger on his soda bottle as it smashed against a garden boulder in the flower bed when he hit the ground. We picked him up, cleaned him up as best we could, and took him home where his mom reassured him that he would survive, calmly placed him in the car and drove him to Dr. Hooper's office, the gash on his finger requiring five stitches.

Sonny was kind, generous, funny, and very creative when it came to the games that would consume our summer evenings outdoors. His imagination and daring had no boundaries and when Bucky first dared us to ride our bikes down the red clay road to the small cottage near the manor where Tramp lived, Sonny was the first to give it a try.

Many evenings our play began with such a dare: one of us riding off the asphalt road, through the dense stand of pine trees, and along the darkening dirt road that led to Tramp's cottage. The one who rode the closest to Tramp's front door would mark his spot in the clay with a Confederate flag tied to a stick and, if he were truly brave, would sound a whistle to stir Tramp out into the open. Bucky, always tempting fate, had gone the closest to Tramp's door. Tramp, his nappy, dark hair glistening against the rising moon and his eyes red with rage, had chased Bucky through the towering pines and out onto the paved road waving a boat oar over his tall, muscular frame. The rest of us shrank behind the trees, mummified with fear until Tramp, mumbling to himself, retreated into the darkness of his home.

Chapter 7

The Rays

BUCKY'S FATHER, Pete Ray, had nick-named him Bucky when he was a toddler and it suited him. Bucky was tough, athletic, daring, quick-to-anger, darkly handsome, and sometimes a little cruel. He adored his father, Pete, whose own tough exterior belied the scars within him. I overheard Mrs. Tinsley whisper to my mother one day as they chatted across the clothesline that Pete Ray's father had been a violent alcoholic who abused him and his mother. Ironically, Pete's father was also a well-respected lieutenant with the Chesterfield County Police Department and a deacon in his church. Bucky, through heredity or intention, mimicked his father Pete's walk and mannerisms, the way he spoke, even the way he smiled. While he idolized his father, he tried to steer clear of his grandfather, Lieutenant Ray, whenever he could.

One day last spring, three school buses serving our side of town pulled up behind each other at the corner of Branch Creek and Kildare, like cars in a circus train. The first one was the rickety old bus with broken seat springs and sticking gears that Mr. Bottoms drove for Sacred Heart Parochial School. Spilling out the side of the bus as the wheels ground to a halt were Charlie, Karena, and I. The bus behind us, sleek and new, was from Branch Creek Elementary, the county public school. Will, Bucky, and Sonny flew through the doors as soon as they opened, talking loudly about spring training, the New York Yankees, the Brooklyn Dodgers, and the Washington

Senators. Behind them, a third bus from Beulah Elementary stopped to unload two dark-skinned Negro girls, who appeared to be about the same ages as Karena and I. Heads down, they walked quietly toward the rickety porch of their bungalow, a relic from the 1920's when Branch Creek Manor was still a working farm and a few such houses sat opposite the manor and across Branch Creek Road. The older of the two glanced back shyly toward Charlie and me. A slight smile crossed her lips as our eyes met and I smiled back, tentatively, but no words were spoken although I felt there was something eerily familiar in her smile, her face. Turning, she rushed on to join her sister who climbed the sinking steps leading onto her porch. I felt both a compassion for and a connection to them though I wasn't sure why. The memory of that moment stayed with me as well as the moment that followed.

As we crested the hill of Kildare, Bucky, who had been deep in conversation about baseball, grew silent as he noticed that his father's Plymouth was parked in front of their house at the end of the street. Glancing at his watch, he knew it was too soon for his father's shift at DuPont to be over. Puzzled, Bucky dashed past all of us anxious to see why his dad was home so early. Excitedly, he ran into the house slamming the screen door behind him, the crash of the door against the sill echoing the sound of Mr. Ray's revolver as he pulled the trigger ending his own life and changing Bucky's forever.

The events of that day will play in my head eternally, a surreal recollection of all that was evil and all that was good in the world, all that we as children would come to learn each in our own way and in our own time.

Hearing the gunshot, neighbors ran out their front doors toward the street. Mr. Goode and my dad were home from their morning shifts at DuPont and the newspaper. Reverend Angstrom had taken a day off to work in his garden. Seeing a bloodied Bucky standing outside his front door, Dad ran back into the house to call the Chesterfield police and Forest View Rescue Squad. Stunned neighbors, realizing what had happened, stepped aside as the old Buick hearse the rescue squad had converted into an ambulance approached within minutes, appearing at the top of Kildare, heading for Bucky's house. Watching the rescue squad pile out of the ambulance and run into the Rays' house, our neighbors began to grieve openly, some with anger and some with regret.

"He just couldn't quit drinking," said Mr. Goode, Pete's coworker at DuPont, as the squad assessed Mr. Ray's condition. "It consumed him. It cost him his job. I tried to talk to him, even told him about my sot of a brother whose wife left him and whose children won't have anything to do with him. Told him he needed to get help. Told him about AA. But no, what does he do? He gives up. He says it's hopeless. He takes everything into his own hands and sends himself off into a self-inflicted eternal sleep leaving his family to clean up his mess. Damn it and damn him!" said Mr. Goode as he covered his face with his hands and wept openly, something I was shocked to see this tough Yankee do.

"But I should have seen it coming," said the Reverend Angstrom, wringing his soil-covered hands. "He had become more and more isolated and unresponsive. The signs were all there. I should have seen them. I should have done more to help him. I offered to take him and his whole family to church, but he said he had no use for church folk. None whatsoever!"

We all stood by in stunned silence as the ambulance workers carried Bucky's father out the front door and down the front steps, placing him roughly in the back of the ambulance. I heard my mother praying softly, her voice cracking with each word: "Eternal rest grant unto him, O Lord."

"Amen," I whispered.

The look on my father's face that day, as he watched Mr. Ray's body being loaded into the ambulance, startled me, sending a shiver down my spine. Was he reliving what he saw in Korea? Could he not let go of those memories? Deep down, on some level, I feared that in time I might come to know what it meant.

Bucky stood apart from his mother, from all of us, tearless, arms rigid by his sides, his fists clenched, as the doors to the ambulance closed. His face, shirt, and hands were scarlet with his father's blood. He watched his father leave him with no lights flashing, no siren blaring, and no goodbye. His mother wept uncontrollably, one arm around Gracie, Bucky's little sister, the other reaching for Bucky, trying to pull him back, but he would not be touched. Mr. and Mrs. Angstrom and my mother and father tried to comfort Mrs. Ray, my mother sweeping Gracie up into her arms and away from the scene as the adults talked about what arrangements needed to be made. They would intervene many times with both Bucky and Gracie over the next year, becoming their extended family whenever Mrs. Ray spent time at Eastern State

Mental Hospital in Williamsburg, the loss of her husband and the burden of raising two children alone widening the crack in her already fragile constitution.

Climbing the stairs to my room that evening, my arms and legs felt as heavy as rain-soaked logs. I crawled under the sheets, closed my eyes, and covered my mouth with my hand to stifle the scream I felt growing inside of me. I could still see a bloodied, hollow-eyed Bucky standing stiffly before me, his fingernails tearing bloody holes into his palms as he clenched his fists by his sides. I hurt for him and Gracie, but also for myself. What would happen to me, to my family, if our father left us suddenly as Bucky's father had? And this night, I heard my dad make more than one visit to the kitchen cabinet to get the Jim Beam he had hidden on the back of a shelf. Finally, I drifted off to sleep, although a fitful one, only to wake the next morning with all the sorrows of the day before still settled on my chest like an anvil. I threw back the covers and swung my legs over the side of the bed. Looking through my window, I could see the day would be sunny and dry, a break from the April showers that had been interrupting our play. I would get ready for school, pushing the weight of sorrow aside, pressing forward into the day.

This is the day the Lord hath made, I reminded myself as my bare feet hit the cool pine floor. And with anger, and shame, I even thought, *I hope He does a better job of it today!*

Bucky was never the same. His once fiery, mischievous eyes became dark and brooding, much like his father's, his stone-like exterior impenetrable and cold. He was like a tomb, silent and sealed. Yet, I always feared that one day his entombed rage would explode, shattering everyone and everything in his path. For now, he could handle anything anyone could dish out, or so it seemed. And except for Bucky, whose home life was as public as he was private, we each assumed the others' lives were worry-free. The evenings we spent together were adventure for some and escape from reality for others, a chance to enter a different realm of existence, to put aside that which we could not control and to experience freedom as only a child could.

Chapter 8

The Incinerator Building, McGuire Veterans Hospital

NATE GLANCED UP AT THE CLOCK as he removed from the hospital refrigerator a burn bucket containing an amputated arm, the last of the day's body parts sent by surgery to the incinerator building for disposal. It was almost time to knock off work, he thought, but he wanted to make sure the fire did its job before heading home. He lifted the severed arm from the bucket and placed it gently into the roaring furnace. Infection following surgery on a mangled hand had taken first the veteran's hand and then his arm. Even penicillin, that wonder drug that saved lives and prevented amputations during WWII, was not effective against the wet form of gangrene that crept into his wounds and ate away at his flesh. Watching the flesh melt away from the bone in the fire, Nate was transported to Korea where he served as a medic in the Army. He poked at the ashes dismissing the splinters of bones to the back of the pit. This was not new for him. He had seen battlefields separate his comrades from their arms and legs, their faces, even their minds. He had been scarred, too, in a way less visible but just as devastating. He preferred the solitude of his little cottage and the quiet drone of evening falling across the landscape to the rowdy times others enjoyed at local night spots. He could not distinguish in his mind the loud music of the clubs from the pounding artillery noise still in his head. And while others partied, he buried himself in his books, enjoying the company of Janie Crawford and Tea Cake in Zora Neale Hurston's *Their Eyes Were Watching God* or even seeing himself in Ralph Ellison's *The Invisible Man*.

It would be good to walk out into the cooling evening air, cross the railroad tracks, and settle into his cottage near the manor. He wiped the perspiration from his brow, gathered his lunch pail and books, and walked out the door and across the lawn of the VA hospital. Just a short way across the Boulevard and through the woods and he would be home.

After all this time, he still missed the sight of his mother pushing open the screen door, the light from the kitchen outlining her ample silhouette as she welcomed him home at the end of the day. When she passed, a piece of him left with her. He had read John Donne and understood deeply for whom the bell tolls. Korea, the battlefields, the butchery of war, diminished him even more. He had grown up in this cottage while his mother tended to the manor and its occupants. Rather than attending Manchester High School with other young people from the county, Nate graduated from George Washington Carver High School, a county school for Negroes, finishing second in his class and first on the track. He immediately enlisted in the army during the Korean crisis, a postscript to World War II and the first real skirmish of the Cold War, hoping to become a medical corpsman. Eventually, he planned to pursue his education using the GI bill to study medicine. He wanted to help repair the ravages of war and disease. Instead, he was relegated to the custodial task of disposing of what war had extracted from humanity.

His mother's death after his return from Korea in 1952 had been devastating for him. She had always suffered with a bad heart and he had lived with the fear of the inevitable from the time he was a small boy and found her unconscious, one hot summer day, on the path between their cottage and the manor, freshly ironed shirts spilling out of a large wicker basket on the ground beside her. She had hung on long enough, though, to see her son walk through the fields and up to her door when his tour of duty was over. It was then that she showed him papers from the last owners of the manor deeding the little caretaker's cottage to her and her descendants. It was not part of the manor and all its acreage when it was sold. When she passed on, it would be his home to do with as he pleased.

He buried her outside the wrought iron cemetery fence, near the giant oak tree, across from the manor where she had served until it was sold. He planted her favorite flowers there: red tulips, sunny yellow daffodils, and pink peonies for the spring; shaggy-faced, rusty-colored dahlias and black-eyed Susans for the summer; and for the fall, large yellow chrysanthemums. A camellia bush he planted shaded her stone, its shiny leaves catching the sun, its blossoms strewing pink petals across her name.

On his return from Korea, he began renovating the cottage starting at the roof, repairing leaks using buckets of tar he pulled up by a rope after climbing on top of the roof. Next, he replaced gutters and downspouts, sending all the rain water into an underground barrel, an extra source of water other than the well that stood in the front yard. He installed indoor plumbing in the kitchen, secretly connecting with the water line from the manor and made part of the back porch a bathroom, a convenient spot for washing up from his outdoor work before heading into the cottage. He left the outhouse standing beyond the back door to remind him of how things had been for his mother and him growing up in the cottage. At the end of each day, he gathered his tools, lay them neatly on his work bench, washed the day's grime off his hands and face, and prayed those annoying kids would not come out as the sun went down.

Chapter 9

Sunday, August 7, 1955

UNROLLING THE HEFTY SUNDAY EDITION of the *Richmond Times-Dispatch* and spreading it across our living room floor, I looked for my father's byline under each photograph. Upon his return from Naval Photography School in Pensacola during WWII, my father left his job with the Chesapeake and Ohio Railroad and became a news photographer for the *Richmond Times Dispatch*, the morning paper, and the *Richmond News Leader*, the evening edition. During his tour in Korea, he had photographed horrific black and white images of war, which he never allowed us to see, keeping his files under lock and key in a Lane cedar chest at the foot of his bed. I overheard him tell Mr. Tinsley that he even had photographs of a policeman roughing up a Negro man brought into the police station because he had sat down in the first available seat on the bus, rather than heading to the rear.

He had a real flair for photography, a trade he was introduced to as a young boy by his Uncle Luke, an itinerant photographer who moved around the Southeast with his black and white pinto pony, a supply of child-size cowboy hats, kerchiefs, and chaps, and his Speed Graphic camera. Mostly, my father helped his uncle with the pony, but he also learned something about printing photos from plates, the preferred method for photojournalists when the pressmen were ready and the deadline for the next edition was at hand. He learned to mark each plate with a grease pencil, noting the subject and date. Later, as a news photographer, he would shoot the morning's assignments, heading back to the paper's dark room to print those photos needed for the *Richmond News Leader*. Then he would head out to capture the afternoon's assignments, readying them for the next morning's edition of the *Richmond Times-Dispatch.*

His uncle had taught him how to charm the young mothers into having their children photographed and how to pose the children and coax them into smiling, skills that would come in handy over the years as he photographed debutantes, socialites, governors, politicians, presidents, law enforcement officers, and even the highly-respected evangelist Billy Graham.

Nothing exciting as far as pictures was in this Sunday's paper, his byline only under photos of teens modeling black-watch-plaid Bermuda shorts in the Miller & Rhoads Tea Room.

There was one article that caught my eye, though. In 1951, students at the Moton High School for Negroes in Prince Edward County, Virginia, had protested the deplorable conditions existing in their school. They had been led by a brave young student named Barbara Johns. Their case went all the way to the Supreme Court which ruled in 1954, according to the article, that racial segregation in public schools was unconstitutional. I thought of the two young Negro girls who lived up the road and wondered how this would affect them – as well as the rest of those attending public schools in Virginia.

"Come on, honey, put that paper away, wash the newsprint off your hands, and get ready for church," my mother said as she finished brushing out Karena's tangled curls.

Folding the newspaper neatly and setting it on the coffee table, I slid off the couch, washed my face and hands, and headed for the front door. Dad was still working that morning so my mother, Karena, and I set out on foot for the 9:00 Mass at McGuire Veterans Hospital Chapel.

Father Karl, a priest who taught German and Latin at Benedictine High School, an all boys' Catholic military school in the city, always seemed to be sleepwalking through Mass. His bushy gray eyebrows hung heavily over his eyes, his chin nearly resting on his chest, his voice droning in the heat. Karena and I found it difficult sometimes to decipher his words or even to distinguish the Latin parts of the Mass from the English. Or maybe he had lapsed into German, thinking he was in front of his class. He must be like Albert Einstein, we thought, so brilliant that he always appeared to be in a fog. In spite of all of that, his sermons were relevant and reverent and even funny sometimes.

Waiting for the punch line to a story is what kept us listening. I always became distracted by the veterans, though, who rolled into the chapel in their wheelchairs, wondering to myself how they were injured and when - Korea, WWII, WWI? Ramps through a covered corridor from the hospital wards allowed patients on gurneys and paraplegics in wheel chairs to enter the chapel without having to go outside. During communion, Father Karl approached each patient solemnly across the back row of the church and presented the Body of Christ to veterans lying on their stomachs, their heads raised up briefly to receive the extended Host. How many had he taught, I wondered, and how many more of both former and future students from Benedictine High School would come to receive communion from him while recuperating from war wounds at the VA?

On this particular Sunday morning, Bucky and his little sister Gracie were crowded in with the Angstrom boys at Branch Creek Southern Baptist Church, their mother away at Eastern State Hospital again. They had gone apprehensively, their father's negative comments regarding church folk echoing in their ears. That evening, Helen Angstrom filled them up with roast beef, sweet potatoes, and corn before releasing them to their evening activities, Gracie learning to crochet and Bucky heading outside to play.

As soon as I could be excused from the dinner table, I headed for the front stoop and sat on its warm cement surface, propped my elbows on my knees, rested my chin in my hands and watched with fascination the aerial ballet being performed before me as bats and moths flew erratically in and out of the cone of light the corner streetlamp began to splay across the street's tarred surface. Crickets chirped, frogs croaked, and voices droned through the opened windows in the still air. I strained to listen for familiar voices through the din of adult admonitions to clean up this, put away that, yes, you may be excused. Closing my eyes, I inhaled the commingled smells of Sunday dinners, cigarette smoke, and bourbon wafting through window screens into the warm air.

Looking back through the front window, I saw Dad, home

from his shift at the newspaper, resting in the Morris chair, Mickey Spillane's *Kiss Me, Deadly* sliding off his lap to the floor as his eyes closed and he breathed softly, sleeping, and maybe dreaming about Mike Hammer's way of taking the law into his own hands. I often wondered if Dad's work as a photojournalist influenced his reading choices or if the books he read, mostly Spillane's, influenced his work. He always seemed to know the scoop on those in power locally, but was very tight-lipped, giving only a knowing look when a questionable name was mentioned. Years later I would learn that Mickey Spillane's novels were of the genre noire, dark and foreboding stories in the pulp fiction vein. Darkness seemed to weigh on Dad at times, a mood or an attitude, but always with a stoic face which betrayed little. And while Dad snored lightly, Mom, as she did every Sunday evening, sat on the end of the couch, her head bent over the newspaper folded across her lap, working diligently to fill in all the blanks of the crossword puzzle.

AND IN THE COTTAGE in the woods and behind the manor, Nate had dozed off while reading a book, after a Sunday spent painting the bedroom walls in his mother's old room.

CHARLIE, AS USUAL, was the first to run up the small grassy incline from her yard to mine, wiping the crumbs from the cornbread she had just stuffed into her mouth onto the seat of her shorts as she slid next to me on the stoop.

"Finished *The Secret of the Old Clock* at rest period this afternoon," she said handing me the Nancy Drew book.

"You know I've already read it. I was the one who told you to read it," I told her with feigned exasperation.

"Look inside, you ninny," whispered Charlie.

Folded in quarters were pages torn from "True Confessions" magazine, a story about a woman who left her husband and ran off with the Jewel Tea man.

"Where did you get this and who would do such a thing? Have you seen Mr. Kruschensky? He looks like Mr. Peepers!" I said to Charlie.

"Not our Jewel Tea man, imbecile," said Charlie with a sigh. "Who would want to write about him?"

. "The Jewel Tea man in this story looks like James Dean, if you can put those two images together."

"Okay, okay. But where did you get this?"

"I found a stack of "True Confessions" and "True Romance" magazines hidden under the metal tray in the bottom of the ice cream freezer when I restocked it with Nutty Buddies. Nadine and Nora were the last to stock it. I think they have been hiding them there so Mom wouldn't see them, but I doubt they'll tell on me about tearing out one story. They'd be telling on themselves," she laughed.

"Shhh, here come Bucky and Will," I said to Charlie as I shoved the article into the book and set it behind a pot of petunias on the stoop. "I'll look at this later."

Bucky and Will appeared at the end of our walkway, the two

of them looking as if they could be beamed up into a space ship by the cone of light from the streetlamp behind them.

"Here come Flash Gordon and the evil Dr. Zarkov," said Charlie under her breath.

"Forget that. The only thing those two have on their minds is the upcoming World Series," I whispered to Charlie. "They love those Yanks and Dodgers."

"But it's the Yankees and the Dodgers! Who below the Mason-Dixon line cares?" wailed Charlie. "It's not the Washington Senators, for crap's sake!"

While I scanned all the pages for my Dad's photos, Charlie read the Sports Page of the *Richmond Times Dispatch* every day. She knew all the major league baseball players, their stats, and what positions they played. Her collection of baseball cards rivaled any of those belonging to the boys in our neighborhood or at our school. She and her dad spent many an evening in the bleachers at Parker Field watching our own Richmond Vees play. And unbeknownst to her, I was a huge Dodger fan like Bucky and held Jackie Robinson in high regard.

Sonny was always the last to arrive, not because he had chores to do but because he was spellbound by the TV and lost track of time. When the five were all assembled, we began to plan the evening. As usual, it would start with a dare: "I dare you to crawl into the window of the manor, go down into the basement, and then . . . I dare you to set a penny on the railroad track, wait for the caboose to pass and then. . . I dare you to ride your bike all the way to Tramp's door and then. . ."

We were not the only ones planning an evening of excitement under the August moon. Nora Tinsley had slipped out her back door to meet an older neighborhood boy, Sam Winston, along the edge of Branch Creek. Sam Winston, with his slicked back hair and troubled gaze, was as close to James Dean as Nora would get.

Having an identical twin had its advantages. Nadine reluctantly agreed to cover for Nora, playing both girls to her parents, slipping in and out of rooms calling to Nora and then answering for her.

"You are going to get in trouble, Nora," she would say.

"And if Dad finds out, neither one of us will ever hear the end of it."

If Charlie had not been with us, she would have caught them. She knew them like the back of her hand and always had her antenna out for their schemes.

"More to blackmail them with," she would have said.

Mr. Tinsley, who had fallen asleep in his recliner, his snores pushing the sports page up and down above his face, would not miss her nor would Mrs. Tinsley who sat near him on the couch, the afghan she was crocheting spilling across her lap onto the floor. No one ever found out what Nora was up to until it was too late.

MEANWHILE, OUT ON BRANCH CREEK ROAD, two young colored girls reached the wrought iron fence of the cemetery. Only one marker was visible beside the overgrown edges outside the fence, an area surprisingly clear of debris, a camellia bush rising above the flat granite footstone with the words Ida Louise Lawrence, 1898 – 1953 engraved at its center.

The older girl lit a candle and held it in front of the marker. The younger girl sounded out the name and asked "Who's that?"

"I don't know," her sister said, "but one day I found a key lying in the grass beside the stone, an old key, the kind used on plantation doors, so I began to wonder if maybe it was a key to the big house up yonder. I was too frightened to take it in broad daylight, so I hid it behind the footstone, right behind the letter "I" for Ida."

Reaching carefully behind the stone, the older girl pulled out the large brass key.

"Oh, no, what are you gonna do? I mean, what are we gonna do?" asked the younger girl.

"Little sister, I'm gonna take you on a tour of
the big house. You ain't gonna believe what's in there."

"How do you know?"

"I already seen it. Came here one night by myself. Lord only knows what we might find."

"Lord only knows what might find us!" said her sister. "I'm scared."

"Come on, little sister, you know I ain't gonna let nothing happen to you."

IN THE SUMMER SKY, a full moon shone across the anxious faces of the five of us, across the manor, across the graveyard, and across the cottage beyond as we left my front stoop, hopped on our bikes, and headed for the street. We needed no flashlights under the glow of that August moon, but, of course, I brought one just in case.

Just to be different, Bucky decided we venture up McGregor Avenue, which began around the curve from where Kildare and Lancaster intersected and continued to form our neighborhood's perimeter where the railroad tracks left off. Bucky always took the lead, followed by Sonny, Will, Charlie, and then me. There was a new family living there on McGregor, the Mierzowskis, immigrants from Poland. Even though their son Leo was a year older than Bucky and Will, he was in the seventh grade with them. When we arrived, Leo was sitting on his front stoop, shaving the bark off a cedar branch with the biggest pocketknife I had ever seen.

"It's not a pocketknife, moron," said Charlie. "It's a switchblade, like the ones in the movies."

Across my mind's eye flashed tee-shirt-and-jean-clad hooligans, raised switchblades glistening in the sun, walking towards one another in an empty parking lot.

"What you guys up to?" said Leo without looking up or stilling the blade.

"Looking for something to do. Got any ideas?" said Will.

"Yeah, I have an idea," said Leo as he flipped the switchblade into the dirt. "Let's have a contest about who can tell the grossest true story," his steely eyes and tight lips conveying a dare he knew he could win.

"Okay, but it has to be true," interjected Charlie. "No made-up stuff, or we will know the difference."

"Okay. I'll go first," I said, mustering my courage and telling the story of my dad stepping in the brown bag of eggs that Mr. Angstrom left on our stoop, describing in detail how my dad cursed as he pulled his yolk-covered shoe out of the bag, yellow ooze dripping everywhere.

"Messy, but not gross," said Charlie who had appointed herself contest judge. "Listen to this one. Kate and I were looking over the fence into Reverend Angstrom's yard while pulling raspberries from his vine. Apron on, Mrs. Angstrom walked from the hen house holding a wiggling, clucking chicken straight out in front of her. She then tucked the hen under her left arm, reached up with her right hand and wrung the chicken's neck. When it stopped squirming, she began plucking its feathers as she walked toward her kitchen door."

"Yuck," I said remembering how matter-of-fact Mrs. Ansgtrom had been about killing that poor little chicken. I did not know at the time that I would be eating its meat in my mom's Brunswick stew the very next day.

Will went next telling the story of how Sonny, seeing my dad cut the tails off the cocker pups with a knife, fainted into his own vomit as he fell, cutting his hand and requiring stitches.

"I got one better than that," said Sonny, trying to move on from Will's story.

"There was this kid at my school in Hoboken who bet the boys at his table that he could swipe a cheeseburger off the cafeteria counter without getting caught. Getting up from the table, he swaggered toward the lunch counter and when the cafeteria lady wasn't looking, he grabbed a cheeseburger off the hot plate, stuffed it down the front of his pants, and sauntered back toward our table, grinning. Suddenly, the expression on his face changed to one of pain, and he ran screaming into the bathroom."

"What happened?" asked Charlie, her eyes wide with anticipation.

"It seems the cheese melted, slid off the hamburger and onto his "thing." The principal, hearing his screams, entered the bathroom in time to see the hamburger bun on the floor and the kid trying to wash the cheese off his you-know-what."

"Oh, no," said Will. "That's disgusting!"

"What's worse," said Sonny, "is that he gained a new nickname he could never shake."

"What was that?" asked Charlie.

"He became known as 'Cheese Balls,' a name he had until he moved to Richmond where nobody knew about it," said Sonny, a twisted grin on his face.

Everyone howled at both Sonny's story and the fact that he told on himself because winning this contest was more important than being embarrassed.

And then we all looked toward Bucky whose eyes were fixated on the ground. Frozen in time he stood, back on that April day when he got off the school bus and ran toward his house. He would not share his story, the one everybody but Leo knew. When he did not raise his head, Leo spoke up:

"My uncle told me that as a young boy in Poland during the

German occupation, he had seen or heard about horrible things done to the Jews or those who hid them. Once, while walking to his house from school, he saw a group of German soldiers begin to harass the Jewish family that lived next door. The soldiers pulled the mother and her baby out of their doorway and onto the sidewalk.

"'Fraulein, you must hand over your baby,' shrieked a lieutenant, pushing his face just inches from hers.

"'No,' sobbed the woman. 'For the love of God, no. I will do anything. Please don't take my baby.'

"When the mother refused to give them her baby, an officer tore the baby from her arms and tossed it high into the air. The mother lurched toward the falling baby, her arms spread out to catch him when another soldier pushed her aside, raised his rifle, and caught the child on his bayonet, piercing the child's chest. The silent baby lay face up, arms stretched out, like the Baby Jesus in the manager, but pierced through with the bayonet.

"'And this is what we do to people who do not cooperate with us,' he said to the mother whose mouth formed the shape of a scream, a silent scream."

"That is the grossest story I have ever heard, but I doubt that it is true," said Charlie, always the skeptic.

"It is true," said Leo. "And then they took the woman, her husband, and the rest of her children and they were never seen again. They died in a concentration camp with hundreds of other Jews from my country."

"How could that happen? I thought camp was a place you went to ride horses and swim?" said Sonny, whose best subject was never history.

Suddenly Bucky's stance thawed and, without saying a word, he climbed on his bike. The tears were coming and he had to get away from all of us lest we should see him in his vulnerable state. By the time we caught up with him, he was barking orders about what games we would play that night starting with a trip to Tramp's house, our need for showing our courage even greater after listening to the Polish boy's story. We biked single file off the asphalt onto the dirt road, a dim light visible in the cottage.

"He's in there," said Sonny. "Looks like he is reading something at the kitchen table."

"Negroes don't read anything but the walls of the post office to see if their pictures are there," said Bucky, who had been spending some time with his grandfather.

"That's not true," said Charlie. "You need to stop listening to your grandfather."

"Whatda' you know?" said Bucky.

I wanted to join Charlie in her rebuke of Bucky, but remained silent. I didn't know what the others would think if I did. Charlie always took the other side, no matter what the argument was. I envied her courage.

This evening would be different. Tramp would not respond no matter how much racket we made. He sat stiffly at the kitchen table, sipping from a brown bottle, his head poised over a book. He never looked away from the book or toward the noise pushing through his window.

Bucky was so frustrated at Tramp's lack of response that he

whistled for all of us to head back to the asphalt road and follow him to the graveyard.

"Get over here, Will," said Bucky. "Let's see how brave you are. Go climb into the manor window by yourself. We'll watch from here. We are going to see who's the bravest and that is your challenge."

"Piece of cake," said Will, although his hands were trembling.

Will walked with his back straight and his eyes on the window with the broken latch. He pushed the window up, crawled inside, and then stuck his head back out the window and said, "Now what? Is that it?"

"Stay put," said Bucky. "I'm sending Sonny on another mission that will make you look like the wuss that you are. When he's done, we'll be back to get you, if you're lucky."

Bucky turned to Sonny and said, "Sonny, you know that incinerator building across the tracks at the VA hospital? The one where soldiers' limbs and guts are burned?"

"Yeah," said Sonny, his feet shuffling nervously.

"I'll bet you won't cross the tracks, walk across the Boulevard, and jimmy the door to that place and go inside."

"Bucky," said Charlie. "Don't you think that is too dangerous for us kids? And what if our parents find out? It will be the end of our games."

"Nothing's going to happen. What could happen?" said Bucky.

"You're nuts," said Charlie. "And you're a fool if you do it,

Sonny."

"Come on, Kate, let's get out of here before something really bad does happen."

"You're such a girl," Bucky called after Charlie as we fled on our bikes.

Before taking off, I slipped my flashlight into Sonny's pocket and whispered, "Wish you wouldn't do this, but I know you will."

Chapter 10

Lost and Found

NATE TURNED FROM HIS BOOK and listened to the stillness of the night. He leaned back in his chair and grinned. Reading about Gandhi made him wonder if a passive approach would be more effective than striking back at his tormentors who, after all, were only children who became easily bored. His plan had worked. The kids had given up and left him to his peace and quiet. He was just beginning to head out on the porch for a breath of fresh air and a smoke when he stopped short, remembering something important he had forgotten to do at work.

"Shit," he said, visualizing the burn bucket with one soldier's amputated foot and another soldier's gall bladder still sitting beside the refrigerator door. When he left work on Friday, he had forgotten to put it to rest inside the Kelvinator, that monstrous steel vessel that housed and cooled the soldiers' parts until they were sent to the oven that would turn them into ashes.

After a weekend in this heat, the stink and the flies will knock me over when I hit the door Monday morning, he thought.

He decided to slip across the tracks, cross the Boulevard, and put the bucket and its putrefying contents into the hulking Kelvinator lest it greet him Monday morning in a most unpleasant way.

In the meantime, the two young Negro girls were rummaging through the attic of the manor, looking for a souvenir by which to remember their adventure. The moon shone through the cracks in the roof, giving them light that was both frightening and welcome. And on the main floor, Will sat motionless in the windowsill, not drawing pictures of what was going on along the streets or dreaming of playing the piano or reading Hardy Boys or even the Psalms, but wondering what he should do next: Run and be proven a coward or stay and face the unknown? And the footsteps he heard above him, he convinced himself, was just the house itself creaking under its own weight.

He wasn't the only one hearing noises. Upstairs the girls stopped their search, both thinking they heard someone moving around.

"I heard something downstairs," whispered Ruby.

"So did I," said Lilly. "I tol' you this was a dumb idea."

"We better get outta' here!" said Ruby, and the two of them slipped down a back staircase and ran across the Boulevard toward the hospital where their mom was working.

Nate reached the incinerator building, unlocked the door, and walked over to pick up the burn bucket sitting next to the Kelvinator. The odor knocked him back, making him nauseated as he opened the Kelvinator's door, set the bucket inside, and then ran, hand over mouth, to the bathroom. In his haste, he had not completely closed the giant Kelvinator door, its light shining down on the bucket inside.

Heaving, Nate threw up in the toilet, the odor from that burn bucket still resting in his nostrils. He took a couple of slow breaths and then pushed open the bathroom door. Looking down, Nate wiped the vomit from his shirt front as he walked back into the room. The watchman, hearing noises, came into the incinerator building from the hospital hallway.

"What's going on in here, Nate," asked the watchman. "What are you doing here? Those kids drive you out of your house again?"

"No, they came around but this time I fixed 'em good."

"Yeah, boy, what did you do?" asked the watchman eyeing Nate with suspicion.

"Just ignored them, that's all. Just ignored them."

"So, what are you doing here?"

Nate explained that he had forgotten to put the burn bucket into the Kelvinator and had come back to take care of it.

"Well, it appears to be taken care of," said the watchman. "So, git on home, boy."

"Yes, sir," said Nate, feigning the politeness that was expected but not deserved. "Yes, sir."

As Nate walked out the door, he noticed a flashlight lying on the ground, its light streaming across the dusty earth.

That watchman must have dropped this on his way in, he thought to himself, as he picked up the flashlight, turned it off, stuck it in his pocket, and headed home.

AS ALWAYS, THE FIVE OF US were to meet on my front stoop before going our separate ways at the end of the night's adventures. Charlie and I got there first. Next came Will and then Bucky who had waited at the graveyard for Sonny to return.

"Sonny hasn't gotten back yet?" asked Bucky.

"No, we haven't seen him."

"He is such a coward – probably hiding out somewhere inventing a wild story to impress us" said Bucky. "Or he might be in trouble somewhere," said Bucky, showing just a hint of concern or maybe even responsibility.

"He didn't have to do it if he didn't want to," said Charlie. "You didn't make him go."

But you made it awfully hard for him not to, I thought.

"Maybe we should check the railroad tracks to see if he got stuck there," Will said. "Remember the time my foot got wedged under the rail and we got it out just before a train came?"

With that, we all ran back up the street, back through the graveyard, and down to the tracks. There was no sign of him.

"I think we should go to the Boulevard and make sure he didn't get hit by a car trying to cross at night," I said.

"We would have heard sirens," Charlie said breathlessly.

"But suppose he was thrown to the side of the road?" said Will. "He could lie there injured for days and we would never find him."

"Or suppose gypsies picked him up and carried him off," I said.

"Okay, that's enough. Let's go," said Charlie, rolling her eyes at what she thought was my preposterous suggestion involving gypsies.

"Coming, Bucky?" she asked as we saw the terrifying realization in his eyes that something might have happened to Sonny.

The four of us ran through the woods to the Boulevard, looking for some sign of Sonny along the way. Nothing.

We crossed the Boulevard and walked to the incinerator building at the VA. Bucky even tried the door, but it was locked and there was no sign of anyone trying to break in.

When we got back to my front stoop, Bucky knew we had to alert our families that Sonny was missing. He made us swear that we would not tell them of his dare. We had checked the incinerator building and it was obvious to us that Sonny had not made it that far. We needed to look elsewhere.

Terrified, we went home to tell our parents that Sonny was missing, truly missing, not hiding in one of our games. We confessed about our games and the dangerous routes we sometimes took to fill up our evenings, all except Bucky's dare that Sonny enter the incinerator building. Word spread rapidly and neighbors came out into the darkness to help with the search. Mom consoled Sonny's mom, reassuring her that he would turn up any minute while Sonny's dad headed across the tracks to search inside the large boxy concrete septic tanks lined up at Layton and Boyd's Septic Tank Company on the Boulevard right behind our neighborhood. It would be a perfect place to hide, he thought. Maybe he climbed in and could not get out. Dad, Reverend Angstrom, and Mr. Tinsley split up and searched the three main streets - Kildare, Lancaster, and McGregor. No one had seen him. It was time to call the police. Bucky's grandfather, Lieutenant Ray, was the first to arrive, asking questions of the parents while looking suspiciously at the four of us.

I could understand how harsh Lieutenant Ray could be simply by looking into his eyes. *Keep it together,* I thought, *just keep it together*. I watched my own father look knowingly at Lieutenant Ray, and it wasn't a look of approval.

Monday came and still no sign of Sonny. Dads drove off to work, looking along the way for any sign of him.

NATE, TOO, HEADED TOWARD WORK, walking through the woods, crossing the railroad tracks and the Boulevard, arriving at the incinerator building. Opening the door, he glanced at the burn schedule for the week posted on the wall. Amputations and surgeries scheduled that week would make Wednesday the first burn day. No body parts would be received until then. Nate, instead, would spend Monday and Tuesday catching up on clerical work.

LIEUTENANT RAY, having learned about our evening games when he questioned our parents, requested to speak with each of us. He asked us about some of our adventures. Will went first telling how we rode to Tramp's cottage, taunted him, and how he had not chased us as he usually did. I was next and told of the bet with Leo on McGregor Avenue about who could tell the grossest story. I also mentioned I had given my flashlight to Sonny that evening in case he needed it. Charlie's story was of seeing eyes looking back at her one evening from the windows of the manor, even though she had said at the time that she did not see them. Bucky came last, his fists clenched beside his legs as usual, his story also of our riding to Tramp's house and how irate he had become the many times he chased us away.

Tuesday and still no sign of Sonny. Forty-eight hours had passed and we knew the chances of finding him alive were lessening. But still, we continued to look . . . and pray.

Lieutenant Ray decided to check the manor for any sign of Sonny. His officers searched its grounds, the cemetery, and then around the caretaker's cottage. Again, nothing.

NATE ARRIVED AT WORK early on Wednesday, knowing much needed to be done to prepare for the burn. The incinerator needed to be stoked, the heat intense in order to make ashes quickly of the burn bucket's contents. When Jesse, an orderly, brought him a burn bucket, Nate quickly fed its contents to the flames. He chatted with Jesse, who had also served in Korea and bemoaned the fact that, as a Negro, jobs for him still were of the servant kind, just as they had been for his ancestors. Nate nodded in agreement as he walked to the Kelvinator to retrieve the burn bucket he had placed there on Sunday evening. He pulled open the wide Kelvinator door, peered inside for the burn bucket and saw instead the body of a young boy curled into a ball, blue and breathless, his mouth opened wide in a frozen scream. The burn bucket with the amputated foot and gallbladder tipped over onto the floor, spilling its bloody cargo across Nate's shoes. Jesse, stepping forward to see what had happened, gasped in horror at the sight of the young boy and took off running through the hospital hallway, hollering for someone to call the police. Nate stood frozen in place – and time. Soon, sirens were screaming up the Boulevard.

Lieutenant Ray, Bucky's grandfather, was the first on the scene. He looked at Nate, poking his chest repeatedly with his forefinger while saying, "Nigger, you're not getting by with this." A deputy handcuffed Nate and shoved him into the squad car.

"We were headed to your address with a search warrant when the call came in." he said.

A search of Nate's cottage turned up Sonny's flashlight. Bucky's grandfather had also spoken with the watchman, who saw Nate at the incinerator building Sunday night. He, too, would testify against Nate and how he had been at the incinerator building on a night he should not have been. Nate also had told him that as for those kids, "he had fixed them good." And in his and Bucky's grandfather's minds, the flashlight and the comments were enough. They had found the murderer.

Thursday morning's *Times Dispatch* reported the finding of the body of a young boy in the incinerator building at the VA hospital. No names, no other info. The *News Leader* that afternoon filled in the blanks showing a recent school picture of Sonny Goode, the now-found missing child. And alongside it was a photo of a handcuffed Negro named Nate Lawrence being thrown into the back of a squad car. That picture sealed his fate in the minds of almost all who saw it.

IN A TINY BUNGALOW with creaky front steps along Branch Creek Road, Ruby and Lilly watched their mom's eyes widen as she read the paper, seeing the picture on the front page.

"Oh, dear Lord. This just ain't possible. This can't be. He a good man. He wouldn't hurt nobody!"

She began to sob and Lilly reached up to console her saying, "Momma, it'll be okay cuz' Ruby and I saw" . . . but before she could finish, Ruby grabbed her by the arm, pulled her through the front door, and sat her down on the steps out of earshot of their mother.

"Ain't you gonna tell what we saw?" said Lilly, who as the younger child was not so aware of how their stories would not be thought credible.

"We need'a think 'bout this carefully," said Ruby, knowing there was much more at stake than Lilly could understand. "Who gonna believe us anyway?"

BACK ON KILDARE AVENUE, Charlie and I sat on my front stoop. Looking across at Sonny's home was painful for both of us. He just couldn't be gone. And Charlie gasped when I showed her Tramp's picture on the front page of *The News Leader*.

"That's Tramp!" she screamed.

"Seems his name is Nate Lawrence, not Tramp."

Will and Bucky, who pulled up on their bikes, had already seen the newspaper at home.

"Do you think he did it?" I asked them both.

"I wonder," said Will, "if those sounds I heard in the manor that night was actually Sonny hiding from us or if someone else was there."

"Maybe it was those dark eyes I saw through the windows that day," I said.

"Don't be silly," Charlie said, though she had seen them, too.

As frozen and heavy with grief as we were, we knew we had a responsibility to discover the truth, wherever it would lead us, because it was our games that led to Sonny's death. That part of our summer was over, our parents' prudent decision. In fact, we were not allowed to go off my front stoop – no Saturday movies, no trips to Harry Accashian's Market, not even bike rides up and down our street. School would start in a few weeks and maybe then we could begin our search for answers.

Chapter 11

September, 1955

JUST AS THEY HAD LAST SPRING, three school buses pulled behind one another on Branch Creek Road: The streamlined Chesterfield County bus from which Bucky and Will departed, the rickety Sacred Heart School bus delivering Karena, Charlie, and me, and the third bus from Beulah Elementary, the two Negro girls descending its steps as they looked knowingly at all of us, a look that again puzzled me.

Much had changed for all of us since that Sunday in August. Sonny's parents grieved guardedly, awaiting the trial of Nate and a sense of vindication. Seeing their side porch without the glider and the TV was just another sign to us that they might be moving on, back north away from the pain-filled reminders.

Nora, Charlie's older sister, was no longer living at home. When her meetings with Sam turned into a "situation," her parents moved her quietly to St. Joseph's Home for Unwed Mothers in Northside while staying focused on the best possible solution for all of them. Word got around and soon all of us knew what had happened. When Nora returned the following summer, there would be a new addition to the family, a beautiful baby boy, Mrs. Tinsley saying she had been taking Lydia Pinkham Menopause Pills which had a reputation for having a "baby in every bottle." Everyone went along with it and Mr. Tinsley finally had that "son" he so wanted. And to Nadine, Nora, and Charlie, he was the "brother" they never had.

The first few weeks of school is mostly review, at least that was the rationale we used in getting our parents to let go of us a bit so that we might venture out further than our front doors. And, thinking the killer had been apprehended, they relented and slowly began letting us ride our bikes to the market, go to the movies on Saturday, and spend some time in the evenings together, as long as homework was done.

AT THE VA HOSPITAL, those who knew Nate began to do their own investigations, quietly among themselves, of course. Ruby and Lilly's mother, Cora, and Jesse, the orderly who was with Nate when Sonny's body was found, began to eavesdrop on conversations, rummage through logs and other papers when no one was looking trying to see who else could have been involved. Even the watchman who would testify against Nate could be a possibility, they thought, his boasting that his evidence, seeing Nate at the incinerator building that Sunday, hearing him say he had taken care of those annoying kids, would cinch his conviction. He was well known for his racist jokes and attitudes by those with whom he came in contact. Some of the doctors and nurses laughed at his jokes; many did not, however, finding them offensive.

OUR LIVES ON KILDARE began to return to normal, whatever that might be. Charlie and I rode up to Mr. Accashian's grocery each afternoon to get our penny candy and items our moms needed for dinner that evening. And Karena, a little older now, sometimes tagged along. Sometimes Will came with us, but Bucky seemed more distant, less willing to join in.

Chapter 12

Karena Henry

KARENA COULD BE ALL EYES AND ALL EARS whenever she wanted to be. And sometimes, it got her in trouble. Left out of the evening play that began on her front stoop, Karena found her own kind of adventure, sneaking off on her bike to ride up Lancaster, sometimes all the way to Branch Creek Road and on to Accashian's Market, checking the bikes thrown down outside to make sure those who knew she shouldn't be there weren't there, too. Every time she walked through the aisles of canned goods, smelled the fresh bread Mrs. Accashian was baking in the back of the store, or saw stacks of fresh chicken, beef, and pork chops in the refrigerated section, she thought of Sister Celine always telling her to remember the starving Armenians whenever she tried to scrape the rest of her macaroni and cheese into the lunchroom trash. She knew Mr. Accashian was Armenian and thought to herself, but said half out loud, "How could they be starving? They have plenty of food."

Hearing her, Haig Accashian, Mr. Accashian's young son, who was stocking the produce section with oranges, a basket of fresh Carter's Mountain Red Delicious and Granny Smith apples resting in a basket on the floor behind him, whirled around and stepped quickly into the basket, sending apples rolling across the aisle. He was about her age and as feisty as she was. And a bit angry. She giggled as he stumbled, but he never lost his composure or train of thought as he began:

"What do you mean, 'how could they be starving?'" he said. "Don't you know about the Ottoman Turks and how they drove the Armenians to near extinction, starving and butchering them by the thousands?"

"No," replied Karena. "I only know what Sister Celine always told us, that we needed to 'remember the starving Armenians' whenever we didn't eat all our food at lunch."

Karena watched as he picked up the apples, put them back in the basket, and then turned toward her again, his dark, deep-set eyes focused on her face.

"Many people don't know because the Turks have always denied it happened."

"Then how do you know it's true?" she asked.

"Because," he said, somewhat exasperated with her, "my grandparents saw it happening. That's why they left and immigrated to the United States after the massacre began in 1915. Some came to the U.S., some went to Lebanon, but the Turks were a threat to them and others in Lebanon at the time also. That's why there are so many Armenian and Lebanese neighborhood grocery stores and small restaurants here."

Karena then told Haig the story of the Polish boy that lived in her neighborhood who was the winner of the 'who can tell the grossest true story' contest, the contest her sister told her about.

"That was in the 1940's, after the Armenian genocide, when even *more* people were killed but that time it was by Nazi Germany, not the Ottoman Turks. Christians were the main target of the Turks; Jews were the main target of the Nazis."

It, too, was unbelievable savagery and brutality hard to imagine. And, all she could think as he spoke was how could something like either of these things happen.

Sometimes Karena biked in the opposite direction on Branch Creek, away from Accashian's, riding in front of the small bungalows across from the entrance to the subdivision. For some reason, she had no inhibitions or preconceived notions about whom to address and whom to ignore as she passed by. She greeted anyone and everyone.

Passing the bungalows on Branch Creek Road, Karena saw a young Negro girl sitting on her front step. *She looks to be my age,* she thought. *Think I will go say hello.* And so, she did.

Flopping her bike down on the yard in front of the steps, Karena plopped down beside the little girl who was weeping, her head down in her lap, and said, "Hello."

Startled, the little girl looked at her and said, "You not s'posed to be here. You gonna get us both in trouble! Better git yo'self on home, white girl."

"Oh, now I recognize you. You get off that bus from Beulah Elementary with all the Negro kids."

"Whatcha' expect? A desk for me and my sista' at Branch Creek? Go home, stupid white girl!"

Unfazed by the girl's comment, Karena replied, "I have never understood why the kids from all three school buses couldn't go to the same school."

"Dummy, it's called segregation! We not good enough to go to school with white kids."

"That's silly," said Karena. And at that moment Karena decided that segregation, whatever that was, would not be a part of her life.

"My name is Karena. What's yours?"

Raising her head and looking straight into Karena's eyes, the little girl replied, "Lilly. And no jokes 'bout a black-skinned girl being named Lilly. I done heard 'em all!"

Just then, Karena saw Bucky and Will pedaling on Branch Creek toward Lancaster. Quickly, she hopped on her bike, told Lilly she would come back to see her, and rode down Kildare hoping to make it home before the guys arrived at her front stoop.

The following day, Karena looked both ways before descending the steps of her front stoop and saw no one who might question her as to what she was doing. She pulled her bike from behind the shrubs and quietly pushed it down the sidewalk to the street. Once there, she hopped on and pedaled frantically up Lancaster Avenue. She got to Branch Creek Road, turned left, and headed toward Accashian's Market. Again, she scoured the area for bikes of those who might recognize her and then walked into the market. Heading down the bread aisle, she turned to see Lilly and her sister with their mother. She started to speak but, remembering what Lilly had said to her, she just nodded to Lilly and moved on.

Later that day, she once again retrieved her bike from her spot behind the shrubs and headed up Lancaster, this time turning right on Branch Creek, passing by the little bungalow where Lilly lived. Turning down the sidewalk and seeing no one around, she leaned her bike against the creaky front steps and walked along the right side of the house, peeking in windows to see if anyone was at home - no one was in the living room, but she could see Lilly's mom and sister in the kitchen taking a tray of freshly-baked biscuits from the stove, the aroma following her as she quietly eased by them. Staying low, she crept down the back side of the house passing under the kitchen window. Turning down the left side of the house, she saw Lilly stretched out on her bed reading a book. She tapped on the window gently so only Lilly would hear her in this tiny house. Lilly looked up, got up from her bed, opened the window and slid out telling Karena she better go home.

"Can't we just play?" Karena said.

"You de' dumbest white girl! You just don't get it, do ya? Our playing together could cause so much trouble, 'specially since ya'll think that white kid was killed by that black man from the hospital up the road."

"Ah, come on. The older kids won't let me play with them and there are none my age who live nearby. You're the only one."

Looking down, Lilly was obviously considering this fact when her sister Ruby came into the room.

"Lilly," she shouted, reaching through the window to grab her, "you betta get yo' butt inside and tell that white girl to git lost!"

Karena gave her an "I-see-whatcha-mean" look, got on her bike and rode off.

The next time Karena sneaked off to Accashian's she saw that Lilly and her mother and sister were there also. She walked down the soup aisle right beside Lilly and as she did, Lilly slipped a note into her hand. Trying not to give away Lilly's gesture, Karena looked straight ahead and continued down the aisle, heading for the front door. As she passed by the front checkout, Haig pushed a butter mint candy across the counter toward her. She smiled at him and popped the candy in her mouth. He would do this each time she visited the store thereafter, a butter mint shoved across the counter followed by another chapter in the history of Armenia. Some days there would even be a knock on her front door with Haig standing there saying, "Hi, I was just in the neighborhood making a delivery for the store and thought I would stop by and say hello." And again, he would pick up where he left off last time recounting in order the events of the Armenian genocide. Today she was in a hurry, though, and only had time for the butter mint. She waited until she was safely out of sight of those in the market and anxiously opened the note Lilly had written.

"You may not be as stupid as I thought, white girl. Meet me in front of the manor on Saturday afternoon just after lunch. I think we could be friends and have our own adventures, maybe better ones than the older kids."

Meanwhile, the "older kids" continued to meet and plan adventures, but not with the same enthusiasm as before. The target of one of their games was in jail, they had lost Sonny, and Bucky was not himself. Most days he did not even show up. Will, Charlie, and Kate spent more time going over what happened that horrible night than they did seeking new adventures. They were getting too old for silly games, they told themselves, especially ones that could turn deadly. And they were.

Saturday afternoon Karena once again pulled her bike from

behind the shrubs, looked out to see if the coast was clear and headed up Kildare toward the manor. Turning right onto the grounds of the manor, she saw Lilly standing at the edge of the lawn with her hands behind her back. When Karena got to her, Lilly said "You ain't gonna believe what I got."

"What?" asked Karena.

With that, Lilly put her hands in front of Karena's face while holding up a large brass key.

"What's that?"

"The key to the manor," said Lilly with her shoulders thrown back. "Ruby found it one day when we was playing over here and hid it behind the caretaker's footstone. We keeps it there so no one'll know. We use'ta come over here often and go through the house when no one was around. After that kid died, we was too scared to come. Ready?"

"I, I guess so," stammered Karena, making Lilly laugh at her hesitation.

Looking left and right, the two girls walked toward the massive front door, inserting the brass key into the lock, trembling a little as the lock's bolts tumbled and they pushed open the massive creaky door. The musty smell of faded, floor-to-ceiling velvet draperies and tattered upholstery seeped out toward them. Karena's eyes widened at all that the manor owners had left behind: massive pieces of oak and walnut furniture, portraits in oil hanging on the walls, oriental rugs covering the floors. She inhaled what had been and felt its grace, even sensing its occupants, long gone. She and Lilly entered slowly, almost reverently, in awe of all before them -

and in fear of what might be behind them.

Anxious to show Karena the treasure troves that could be found on the second floor, Lilly led the way up the spiraling front staircase, Karena following closely behind her. As she climbed, she told Karena about the day she and Ruby were hunting for treasures in the attic when they were frightened by noises they heard coming from downstairs.

"We ran fast as we could down the back stairway, out the back door, and 'cross the Boulevard. We ran so fast we had'a stop at the incinerator building to catch our breath before heading home."

On hearing this, Karena abruptly stopped following Lilly up the stairs.

"You and Ruby must have been upstairs when Will was downstairs on a dare from Bucky, the same day Sonny disappeared. You must have been the noises Will thought he heard," said Karena.

Lilly spun around as if stung by a hornet and saw the quizzical yet knowing look on Karena's face.

"If you ran toward the incinerator building, did you see Nate there? That watchman said he saw him there," Karena asked.

"I don't know nothin' 'bout Nate," she said as she turned, ran down the stairs past Karena, and out the front door.

"Wait, Lilly. Why are you leaving?"

"I don't know nothin' 'bout Nate," Lilly replied as she hastened her pace, running away from the manor with the same speed she had on the day of Sonny's death, the day that eerie noises from the first floor had sent her and her sister down the back stairway, across the Boulevard, and finally beside the incinerator building. But this time, she ran toward her own little bungalow on Branch Creek Road.

Chapter 13

Sunday, December 18, 1955

KARENA PICKED UP THE SUNDAY *TIMES-DISPATCH* and began scanning the photos on the front page looking for her dad's bylines, just as Kate had always done. A photo, though not one of her dad's, caught her eye. It was of a frightened little girl, eyes wide and teeth clenched, being held on her mother's lap in a doctor's office, a large needle descending toward her arm.

Those darn penicillin shots is what Karena thought, a grimace tightening her lips.

It seemed every time she went to the doctor, whether for a cold, the flu, a toothache, a hangnail, whatever, Dr. Hooper always gave a shot of penicillin. It had become the answer to every health issue. Instead, this shot was for a new polio vaccine developed by a Dr. Jonas Salk, whose picture accompanied the article.

Thankfully, she thought, *while we missed out on playing outside, going to the lake, going to parks, going to the movies, someone was coming up with a solution to the problem even if it means Dr. Hooper will whip out that darn syringe again, jab it into a vial, hold it upright, squirt a dribble of its contents into the air, and then head for us!!*

Another photo on the front page was of U.S. troops arriving in Vietnam to replace the French who had left the conflict there,

Vietnam becoming another phase of the Cold War. The article also referred to the part U.S. troops played in the first phase of the Cold War, the Korean Conflict, as it was called.

Just got out of Korea. Now we are sending troops to Vietnam? This Cold War keeps getting warmer and warmer. Guess we'll be diving under our desks again!

One more. . . a photo of a stately Negro woman named Rosa Parks who on December 1, two weeks earlier, had refused to give up her seat on a bus to a white man in Montgomery, Alabama. She had been sitting in the colored section, but the law said if the white section was full, as it was that day, she would have to relinquish her seat to a white person if asked. She was arrested and fingerprinted, her mug shot on the front page.

Her face was that of a true Southern lady, her best Sunday hat resting on her head, but with booking numbers plastered across the front of her tailored suit as she looked solemnly, even stoically, at the camera.

This could be a photo of Mrs. Angstrom heading out to church. Hat, gloves, tailored suit - only difference – skin color.

When asked by a reporter how she got the courage to do what she did, she calmly replied, "You must never be fearful about what you are doing when it is right."

You must never be fearful about what you are doing when it is right.

Karena couldn't help thinking how brave this woman must be to confront not only a white man on a bus but also a system that seemed so unfair.

Because of her arrest, according to the article, citizens began boycotting the bus system in Alabama. Leading the boycott was a Negro man, a minister named Reverend Martin Luther King, Jr. The Associated Press photo under the headline showed hundreds of people, mostly Negroes and some whites, following behind him through the streets of Montgomery, arm-in-arm and heads held high.

And we still have three school buses arriving each day at the entrance to our neighborhood. Makes no sense.

Turning to the local section, Karena gasped when she saw that her dad had taken a picture of Nate Lawrence at the Chesterfield County Courthouse. Head down, hands cuffed behind him, he was walking into the courtroom escorted by Lieutenant Ray, who held a tight grip on Nate's arm. In the background was the watchman, leaning against the wall with a smug look on his face as he watched Lieutenant Ray shoving Nate toward the courtroom door. Reading on, she learned that his trial would be the week after Christmas. She laid the paper across her knees and looked toward the ceiling in deep thought.

Somebody knows something they're not telling.

Immediately, her last escapade with Lilly came to mind.

SEEING KARENA STARING at the ceiling in deep thought as I walked into the living room, I knew something was up, knew she was carefully planning something that would not be a spontaneous reaction, the norm for her in her younger days.

"What's going on, Karena?" I asked.

"Nothing you could help with," she snapped.

"How do you know that?"

"Because you wouldn't be willing to take the chances to find out what we need to know."

"I, who took part in all those evening adventures while you sat home?"

"I had my own adventures you never knew about," she said, a mischievous grin replacing her scowl. "And besides, you're too much a follower, not a leader."

"Well, give me a chance to change," I said, rolling my eyes at her arrogance.

"Okay," she said. "Okay."

And so she told me what she thought and how we could become detectives, ones that may find out the truth and discover who killed Sonny.

On Monday afternoon, when the school buses were lined up at Branch Creek Road and the students were descending from all three, Karena grabbed me by the hand and pulled me toward Lilly and her sister getting off the last bus to arrive. This time they did not smile, but looked apprehensively at the two of us as we approached. Charlie, Will, and Bucky, staying back, looked on in surprise.

"I know you both know something you are not telling about the day Sonny died," said Karena. I gasped at her gall. She was becoming more like Charlie, who, unlike me, always took the initiative in so many situations.

Lilly looked directly at Karena, a look that revealed the strong, but secret, friendship that somehow had developed between them. Looking down, her chin against her chest, Lilly quietly answered, “Yes.”

“Shut up, Lilly. You know what the watchman tol’ us,” said Ruby as she grabbed her by the shoulder, pulling her away from us.

“Stop it, Ruby,” she said, jerking free of her sister’s grasp.

Standing stiff as a post and looking straight at Karena, Lilly began to speak.

“Ruby and I saw what happened to Sonny. It wasn’t Nate’s fault. In some ways, it was our fault,” she said and then began to sob.

Looking at her face to face, Karena placed her hands across Lilly’s shoulders.

“Well, if it wasn’t Nate’s fault,” began Karena gently, “and you don’t say something, Nate may also lose his life. Remember what Rosa Parks said.”

“What the heck is she talkin’ ‘bout?” said Ruby.

Looking up and holding in her sobs, Lilly turned to Ruby and said, “Miss Rosa Parks said ‘You must never be fearful about what you are doing when it is right.’ We have to do what is right!”

“But the watchman said he would. . .”

“We have to do what is right no matter what happens,” interrupted Lilly.

Ruby sighed in exasperation, looked toward the sky for a moment and then lowered her head and nodded, even seeming somewhat relieved that what they had been hiding out of fear would be out in the open soon. In some ways it would mean freedom for them, too.

That evening, our dad walked up the sidewalk to find Karena and me sitting on the stoop waiting for him.

We followed him into the house and into the bedroom where he slid his heavy camera bag off his shoulder and kicked off his shoes. He hung his sport coat on the bed post, the now-empty flask in his pocket clinking against his keys as he did so.

"We have something to tell you," Karena said.

"Okay, let's hear it," he said as he sat on the bed looking down to take off his socks, never suspecting what would come from our mouths.

"We know some witnesses who can tell a different story of what happened to Sonny, who can explain away the arguments of Lieutenant Ray and the watchman about Nate being Sonny's killer," said Karena.

With the mention of Lieutenant Ray, Dad raised his head and then looked toward the cedar chest at the foot of the bed, thought for a moment, and calmly said, "I'm listening."

When he heard the story, he immediately walked outside, down the slope to the Tinsleys' house and, as we peeked out the window, we saw him with his arms folded across his chest as he spoke with Mr. Tinsley on their front stoop. Mr. Tinsley rolled his cigar from side to side in his mouth, his thumbs tucked under his suspenders as he listened intently to Dad. He then seemed to nod in agreement. Dad turned and headed back up the slope, a determined look on his face.

On the Tuesday after Christmas, Mom, Karena, and I jumped into Dad's Studebaker and rode with him to his newspaper assignment covering the trial of Nate Lawrence at Chesterfield County Courthouse. Behind us, as he had promised Dad, was Tinsley's Rolling Market, bringing Charlie, Will, and Bucky. And not far behind was a small Ford truck driven by Jesse, the orderly who had been with Nate when Sonny's body was found. Cora was in the front seat beside Jesse, her daughters Ruby and Lilly in the truck bed, arms over the sides, hanging on for dear life. Not three school buses, but three vehicles: a Studebaker, a Rolling Market, and a Ford truck, all of whose occupants hoped to see justice done.

Turning onto Courthouse Road, we could see the courthouse looming in the distance, a vision promising justice for victims and victimizers. In some ways, the Chesterfield Courthouse reminded me of the manor at Branch Creek, with its columned façade, historic architecture, wide front entry, and massive door. And like the manor, there was a smaller building nearby, but not a cottage like the one where Nate lived. Dwarfed by the Courthouse, the building, a rustic relic from the 1800's, was the Chesterfield County Jail, its original first-floor exterior of thick, gray granite blocks, its second-floor, a later addition, of smooth red brick. Iron bars formed grates across each window on the upper level, cells for prisoners located there. A dwarf beside a giant. Not the cabin by the manor, but Nate's new home.

Some of us sat and others stood in the back of the courtroom as witnesses were called. First to testify was the watchman who said that he found Nate in the incinerator building on a Sunday night when he shouldn't have been there. When asked why he was there, the watchman said Nate told him he had forgotten to place a burn bucket containing rotting body parts in the Kelvinator. He held his head up as he spoke, looking out over the jury and toward the defense table where Nate sat. He looked so pleased with himself that he had helped to solve this mystery. He almost gloated. He repeated to the jury Nate's answer when he asked him if those kids, one of which was Sonny, had been pestering him again with their evening games. He responded that Nate said, "No, they came around but this time I fixed 'em good."

The jury was visibly stunned on hearing those words.

"You may be excused," said the judge.

Lieutenant Ray was called to the stand. He repeated his story about Nate being in the incinerator building the Wednesday that Sonny's body was found in the Kelvinator. He described how in searching Sonny's cottage, they had found a flashlight, the one that Sonny's friend had given him when he started his adventure the night he disappeared.

Two damning testimonies. Jury members shook their heads.

While the Lieutenant continued his testimony, Dad walked down a side aisle to the front where Nate and his attorney were sitting. His camera and his being a member of the press often got him into places others could not go. Leaning down, he whispered to the attorney, who turned and looked in the back of the courtroom at all of us sitting there.

"Your honor, I would like to request a short recess. I have been made aware of some witnesses we may need to hear."

As it was almost lunch time, the prosecutors, who were sure

they had this in the bag, did not object and the judge allowed a one-hour break.

Nate's attorney met all the kids and their parents in a conference room. He listened intently to each of us tell how that night had played out. Bucky admitted sending Sonny to the incinerator building on a dare just as Will had been sent to the manor where he thought he heard someone walking around upstairs, which he had. And I told of giving Sonny a flashlight while asking him not to take this dare. Charlie nodded in agreement to all we said, adding that she also begged Sonny not to go. Then Ruby and Lilly spoke, at first hesitantly. Karena walked over and put her arm around Lilly as she began to speak as did Ruby. The attorney, stunned by each revelation, nodded with approval as the pieces all came together.

"Will you be okay to repeat what you have told me from the stand?" he asked Ruby.

"I will," she said.

"And you, Lilly?"

Lilly lifted her head and looked straight at Karena who nodded her own head as if to say "You can do this, Lilly."

"Yes," said Lilly.

Karena's confidence has rubbed off on her was all I could think. And it had.

Over the prosecutor's objection, the judge agreed to allow Ruby to testify followed by Lilly. It would be good to have two corroborating witnesses, said the judge, especially given their young age.

The two sisters had witnessed it all and so each had her say.

"I call Miss Ruby to the stand," said Nate's attorney as he shuffled pages of notes he had taken on his meeting with the children.

Ruby walked up the aisle and climbed into the witness chair.

"Tell us what happened the night in question, the night you saw Sonny at the incinerator building."

Ruby began hesitantly, but her voice became stronger as she spoke.

"Lilly and I had snuck into the manor and gone up the steps trying to find treasures there. When we heard noises comin' from the first floor, we ran down the back stairway, out the manor, and raced 'cross the Boulevard toward the hospital to find our mother who was working there. Just as we got close to the incinerator building, we saw one of the white boys that gets off the Branch Creek School bus heading to the door."

"Can you identify 'the white boy' as Sonny Ray?" asked the attorney as he showed Ruby Sonny's school photo.

"Yes, sir. That's the same boy," said Ruby, tears beginning to fill her lower lids.

"Please continue"

"The white boy, Sonny, had a small flashlight in his hand. We ran to the side of the building and looked in the window wondering why the light inside the incinerator building was on when it should'a been off and what would happen if Nate found that kid there."

"And why should it not be on?" asked the attorney.

"'Cuz ain't nobody supposed to be there on a Sunday."

"And what did you see?"

"The white boy must'a got to the front door, found it unlocked, and walked right on in. When he got inside, he saw a light coming from that big refrigerator because its door was slightly open. When he got closer, he pinched his nose like he was smelling something really bad."

"What do you think it was?"

"My momma told me she has'ta carry soldiers' arms, feet, legs, and innards to Nate so he can burn 'em. He puts 'em into the Kelvinator waitin' for a burn day. They begin to rot and smell awful if they don't get into the Kelvinator right away.

"What happened next, Miss Ruby?"

"Just as the white boy got close to the Kelvinator, Nate suddenly stepped out the bathroom. The light was shining down on him. We could see it was Nate. Lilly whispered to me, 'Oh, no, Nate ain't s'posed to be here today. S'pose he sees that white kid!'"

Ruby looked as if she was ready to cry, to lose it completely.

"Keep going, please."

"That white boy saw Nate comin' out that bathroom."

"Did Nate see Sonny?"

"No, 'cause he had his head down wiping something off his chin and shirt."

"What happened next?"

"That white boy saw Nate first when he come out the bathroom. The door to the Kelvinator was just barely open so that white boy, scared of Nate finding him, jumped inside and closed the door behind him. "

"Thank you, Miss Ruby."

The prosecuting attorney rose and walked toward Ruby.

"Just one question, Miss Ruby. What happened to the flashlight you said Sonny had?"

"I guess he put it down when he was tryin' to open the door. Probably had to use both hands to turn the knob. Then, he didn't need it when he got in 'cuz the light was on."

"Did you see anyone there that night besides Sonny and Nate?" he asked.

"Yes," said Ruby.

"And who was that?'

Ruby looked straight toward the watchman and pointing to him said, "He was there, too."

At that point, Nate's attorney asked that Ruby be excused so that Lilly could continue the girls' testimonies.

The prosecuting attorney nodded in agreement and Ruby climbed down from the stand.

Lilly rose from her seat and climbed into the witness chair.

"Lilly, Ruby has told us what she saw that night. Do you agree with all she said?"

"Yes," replied Lilly.

"Since you do agree, can you tell us what happened after Sonny closed himself into the Kelvinator?"

Looking down at her hands folded in her lap, Lilly began: "We saw the watchman come into the building from the hallway. He was talking to Nate and walked with him outta' the door. We heard him say to Nate as he walked out, "Well, it appears to be taken care of, so git on home, boy."

"What happened next?"

"As soon as Nate left, the watchman come 'round the building and found me and Ruby, looking into the window. He crept up behind us and grabbed our arms, jerking us around toward him.

"What did he say to you?"

"He said, 'What you little coons doing here?'"

"What did you tell him?"

"We couldn't tell him we'd gotten scared by noises after sneakin' into the manor and were runnin' to find our mother at the VA hospital and we didn't get a chance to tell him what we had just seen through the window."

"Why is that?"

"He grabbed both of us by our arms, pullin' us down to the ground. He shouted at us, sprayin' our faces with his spit. He said, 'If I catch you snoopin' 'round here again, you'll be sorry! Do you understand me, you little good-for-nothin's? You'll be sorry you ever laid eyes on this place.' He squeezed our arms harder but Ruby tore herself loose. When he reached out to grab her arm again, I kicked him in the shin. As we ran away, he yelled at us, 'I know who you are. I've seen you with your mother at the hospital. If you want her to keep her job, you better keep your black asses off this property.'"

"Did you tell anyone what you had seen?" asked the attorney.

"We was too scared. That watchman was so mean to us."

"Thank you, Miss Lilly," said the attorney.

The judge then asked if the prosecutor had any questions. Looking ill at what he had heard, the prosecutor answered, "No, your honor."

"Miss Lilly, you may be excused," said the judge.

Lilly looked at Nate as she climbed down from the stand. He looked both shocked and relieved at what had he just heard.

The prosecutors had no more questions and no closing argument, so Nate's lawyer began his closing statement, retelling what the girls had seen:

"As Nate was losing his supper in the bathroom, Sonny slowly turned the knob of the incinerator building's door and, to his amazement, found it unlocked. The odor that hit him was not as strong as his concern about his playmates who would never let him forget that he was a coward if he did not push on. Sonny stepped in slowly, cautiously, making his way toward the only light in the room, a light from a huge refrigerator, its door slightly ajar. He moved slowly toward the door and peeking inside found a bucket glistening with a soldier's foot and an unrecognizable, gelatinous mass full of blood, reeking of rot. Covering his mouth and stifling a gag, he looked up to see a tall, dark silhouette emerging from a door into the room, a light shining down on his lowered head. *I need to get out of here,* he must have thought, as he took the nearest hiding place available and crawled inside the Kelvinator and quietly pulled the door closed. He probably thought he could wait until the coast was clear and then he would have a great story with which to show up the others with their games.

"The night watchman appeared on the scene, escorted Nate out of the building, commenting that "it appears to be taken care of" alluding to the burn bucket being placed into the Kelvinator, Nate's reason for being there on a Sunday.

"In those few minutes, the girls and the watchman unwittingly had sealed Sonny's fate. The watchman did not know that Sonny was in the Kelvinator and the girls did not know Sonny could not open the Kelvinator door from the inside. As a watchman, his priority was clearing the grounds of trespassers, like Ruby and Lilly. What would have happened if they had breathlessly told the watchman what they had seen? But his threats terrified them. They ran away. And so, Sonny, in the time it took for the watchman to shoo away the trespassers, suffocated in that air-tight Kelvinator, unable to open the door from the inside."

The watchman looked ill, knowing he might have saved Sonny if he had not made the girls too frightened to speak.

While the jury was deliberating Nate's fate, those who had created the games that led to Sonny's death sat quietly, heads bowed in prayer, thought, shame, or all three. Decisions made; consequences realized.

In less than a half hour, the foreman walked into the court from the jury room. As he moved toward the bench, those waiting for an answer became silent.

The foreman approached the bench and handed the judge the jury's decision.

Looking down at the paper, the judge read the decision to himself, paused before looking up, and handed the paper back to the foreman.

"How do you find the defendant, Nate Lawrence?"

"We find the defendant," the foreman said turning to face Nate, "not guilty."

Nate wept openly, his face buried in his shackled hands. The caravan of truth seekers sitting and standing in the back of the courtroom breathed a collective sigh of relief knowing that an innocent man had been spared and the mystery of Sonny's death had been solved. The children in the courtroom gleefully ran up the center aisle toward Nate who smiled down at them, thanking them while the sheriff unlocked his handcuffs, the flash from my dad's camera capturing the moment. The Goode family, comforted by all who were there, wept openly, relieved their nightmare had found some closure even though nothing would bring Sonny back.

After allowing a moment of celebration, the judge whispered to the bailiff to call the court to order, smiled, and addressed those seeking justice as well as those seeking vengeance.

"I want to thank the children for coming forward today. I know this was difficult for them not only because of their youth, but because they represent a community often divided by race. Hopefully this is a sign of things to come, where we will be one community regardless of color."

Turning toward the parents, he said, "You have raised good, responsible children who are not afraid of doing the right thing. Our future is in good hands. I congratulate all of you."

Not happy with the verdict was Lieutenant Ray who sneered at Nate as he walked out the courtroom, a look that promised "I'll get you next time." When he saw Dad watching him, he stiffened, an odd look that suggested he knew what Dad knew, whatever that was. Bucky looked at his grandfather, Lieutenant Ray, with a face that showed no emotion, neither fear nor anger, only resolve.

Chapter 14

April 5, 1968

KATE'S MOM PUT THE CROSSWORD PUZZLE ASIDE and reached for the newspapers stacked on the coffee table in front of her. She began to sort them by date, those she had saved over the years. Scissors in hand, she prepared to piece together the news - news of her family, her neighborhood, her world.

The headline for this day, April 5, was horrific. Photos of Martin Luther King, Jr., standing on a balcony at the Lorraine Motel in Memphis, Tennessee, just prior to being shot by a sniper covered the front page. According to the Associated Press report, he had been shot around 6:00 p.m. on April 4 and taken to a hospital where he died around 7:00. He was only 39 years old. Setting the paper down, she thought of words Dr. King had spoken in a speech recently, thinking, after seeing this, that they seemed almost prophetic. Looking through the papers of the last few days, she found the article she was looking for containing the words delivered to a huge crowd of striking sanitation workers on April 3, just one day before King was assassinated. Scanning down his speech, she came to the words he ended with. She read them aloud, softly to herself, overwhelmed by both the urgency and the prophesy of his message:

"We've got some difficult days ahead, but it really doesn't matter with me now, because I've been to the mountaintop ... I've seen the Promised Land. I may not get there with you. But I want you to know tonight, that we, as a people, will get to the Promised Land."

God help us, she thought, *difficult days behind us, difficult days ahead.*

Pulling from the stack a June, 1966 Sunday paper, she found the Wedding Section with black and white photos of brides in long, white gowns posted alongside their wedding announcements. Taking the scissors, she began to cut carefully along the edges of one:

The marriage of Miss Katherine Henry, daughter of Mr. and Mrs. James Henry, to William Angstrom, son of the Rev. and Mrs. Miles Angstrom, all of Richmond, took place yesterday at McGuire Veterans Hospital Chapel.

The Reverend Karl Leonard, Chaplain at McGuire Veterans Hospital, officiated, assisted by the Reverend Miles Angstrom, who read the gospel and blessed the couple.

Miss Karena Henry of Richmond was her sister's maid of honor. Reverend Charlene Tinsley, also of Richmond, was a bridesmaid.

George Angstrom of Richmond was his brother's best man. Haig Accashian, also of Richmond, was an usher.

Katherine is a graduate of Westhampton College and teaches English at a local high school. William is a graduate of William & Mary College and is an architect with a local firm. He also plays piano for the Richmond Symphony.

The couple will reside in Richmond.

So much in that announcement, she thought. Charlene, "Charlie," always a devout Catholic and defender of the faith, had studied Theology at Westhampton College, she and Kate sharing rides there each day with a new neighbor who was attending Richmond College, the men's division just across Westhampton Lake. She transferred to Union Theological Seminary in her sophomore year, and, dismayed with her church's failure to ordain women, joined the Presbyterian Church and became one of the first women to be ordained as a minister in Virginia in 1965.

Missing that day was Sonny, of course. From their new home in Corning, New York, the Goodes had sent Kate and Will a wedding gift of Corning Ware Casserole Dishes decorated with blue cornflowers, their way of wishing them well when physically being present there would have been too painful for them. As for Bucky, who had been at the core of all that happened those days long ago, he sadly but heroically died in Vietnam when he shoved another soldier out of the way of an incoming mortar. Tearfully, his mother had accepted a Purple Heart and a Silver Star for his bravery, a now-grown Gracie by her side. He was not drafted as most were during the Vietnam War, nor did he run to Canada to escape the draft, but he had enlisted in the Army upon graduation from high school, much to his mother's dismay. He told her at the time it was a duty he needed to fulfill.

And one more clipping: A photo of Karena beside her engagement announcement in today's paper:

Mr. and Mrs. James Henry announce the engagement of their daughter, Miss Karena Henry to Mr. Haig Accashian, son of Mr. and Mrs. Harry Accashian, all of Richmond.

Miss Henry graduated from Richmond Professional Institute with a degree in Social Work and is employed by Richmond City Schools as a guidance counselor.

Mr. Accashian also graduated from Richmond Professional Institute with a double major in History and Business. He runs Accashian's Markets around the city of Richmond and Chesterfield County.

A late summer wedding is planned.

And finally, a columnist who wrote the "Where Are They Now?" column had featured the story of Nate Lawrence in a 1966 edition of the paper, eleven years after Sonny's death. It was a bio beginning with Nate's childhood in Chesterfield living in the cottage behind Branch Creek Manor; his attendance at Carver High School, the high school for blacks in the county; his tour of duty in Korea working as a medic; his job at the VA hospital managing the incinerator; his arrest and trial for the murder of a young white boy; and his exoneration because of the work of the same neighborhood kids who originally provided evidence that caused him to be charged. After his release, Nate, with assistance from the VA hospital, his employer, along with the GI bill, was finally able to pursue his Doctor of Medicine at Howard University in Washington, D.C., becoming a surgeon working again at the VA hospital, restoring rather than refrigerating body parts. Alongside the article was a picture of Nate leaving the courtroom after his acquittal in 1955 with Ruby, Lilly, and Karena walking beside him, their families following behind. When asked that day about the role the children played both in his being charged and then acquitted, Nate, looking back at their parents, quoted what he said was an old African proverb: "It takes a village to raise a child." Then smiling down at the girls, he added, "But sometimes it's the child that raises the village."

She spread the articles out on the dining room table, keeping them in chronological order. Carefully, she pasted them into a lap-size scrapbook, its brown-tooled leather cover attached to its back with black cord strung through all the pages. She looked through this life one more time, slowly, laughing and crying as she did so. Picking up the scrapbook, she walked into her bedroom toward the end of her bed. She unlocked the cedar chest and gently placed the scrap book inside, being careful not to disturb and not to look at that stack of photos placed there face down by Jim.

More there than I want or need to know, she thought.

It was a beautiful day, an early spring day with daffodils and irises beginning to push through the soil. Grabbing her cigarettes and an iced tea, she opened the front door and headed for the front stoop, the stoop which had been the base for the neighborhood kids' games as well as the setting for family photos. Sitting on its cool surface and looking up Kildare, she watched for Jim who would be returning from his day shift at the newspaper. She sipped her tea and took a long drag on her cigarette, the smoke swirling over her salt and pepper hair. Seeing Jim's car weaving down Kildare, she stood.

The years had been kind,
The years had been cruel,
But they had been
And will be.

ACKNOWLEDGEMENTS

To my family for your support and encouragement, thank you. To the early readers - Greg Martin (co-worker and voracious reader), George Gibrall and our children George, Michael, Mary, Jay, and Catherine - thank you for your input and suggestions. To Ginaree Creamer and Trish Shaughnessy for your laser focus on detail, thank you. To Sandy Shaw, who helped untangle the knot I called a plot in its early stages and to Rosemary Jones Serfilippi, who smoothed out some wrinkles in its later stages, I am forever grateful.

ABOUT THE AUTHOR

Brenda Gibrall lives in Henrico, Virginia, just across the James River from the Chesterfield County described in these pages. Educated at Sacred Heart Parochial School and St. Gertrude High School, she received a BA in English from Westhampton College at the University of Richmond. This is her first novel.

Made in the USA
Columbia, SC
25 May 2020

97835500R00069